Advance Praise

"Kate Kort's second novel, *Laika*, is a chilling yet moving exploration of an embattled girl's plummet into paranoid schizophrenia while living homeless on mean city streets. The novel keeps the reader close via an unexpected point of view, brilliantly rendered. Laika could be one more tragic runaway if not for Graham, a middle-aged man with his own psychic battle and a huge heart, who illustrates the novel's (and life's) greatest lesson: to be decent human beings, we must care for those who suffer, no matter how damaged we are ourselves."

—Susan Swartwout, author of *Odd Beauty, Strange Fruit*

"Kate Kort's *Laika* grabs the reader as few YA novels do. In fact, it transcends the genre by creating two characters—Laika and Graham—who represent the dark side of an American life few like to acknowledge. A street kid haunted by psychological demons, Laika survives by her wits in a world that doesn't particularly care for damaged kids. That is, until an equally damaged adult takes her under his wing. Told in second-person—a point of view that can feel annoying in less skilled hands—*Laika* offers a relevance that seems particularly important now as our health-care system comes into question. We can only wonder how many more Laika's we will see."

—Michael C. White, author of *Resting Places* and *Soul Catcher*

"*Laika* first grabs the reader's attention by its use of a second person point of view, a narrative decision brilliantly suited to convey the thoughts of a fourteen year old devolving into the separations of paranoid schizophrenia. Its fresh take on the picaresque novel shares many of the genre's characteristics, including realistic depictions of street life and its roguish characters, and a protagonist who is sympathetic despite her stealing and lying her way towards continued survival. Ultimately, though, *Laika* transcends any easy demarcations, since it insists we consider how much we will allow the lives of seriously damaged people to impose on our own humanity, and, more importantly, how ready we are to believe in the heroic potential of those suffering from mental handicaps. Without ever straying from its gripping, lyrical realism, *Laika* leads us to not only compassion, but also to admiration and hope. "

—Joe Benevento, author of *Saving Saint Teresa* and *After*

"*Laika* is a force from its start, propelling readers through a story that's somehow both tender and unsettling, mysterious and revelatory, intimate and widespread. If you want complex, intriguing characters with a plot that will keep you guessing, trust me: *Laika* is your next favorite book."

—Anne Corbitt, author of *Rules for Lying*

"Laika Ephrem is a child whose world is darkness and Graham a man who has experienced some darkness of his own. A good-hearted waiter who has seen her stealing food to survive, he knows she's in trouble and he only wants to help. But, Laika's problems are much deeper than finding her next meal, and helping her may be more than Graham can handle. As Laika's tenuous grasp on reality begins to loosen, and the voices in her head urge her toward destruction, Graham must convince her that what she thinks is real is merely an illusion before time runs out.

"In this brilliantly conceived and executed novel, Kort takes her readers into a distorted world where fear and paranoia overwhelm reality. With compassion, honesty, and startling clarity, she convincingly portrays a terrifying affliction and reminds us that human beings dwell behind numbers and statistics and they deserve to have their stories heard."

—Cynthia A. Graham, author of *Beulah's House of Prayer*, *Beneath Still Waters*, and *Behind Every Door*

"In *Laika*, Kate Kort explores the title character's world with heartbreaking clarity. The novel's electric prose and beautifully rendered characters thrum with delicate fear and sadness as readers bear witness to Laika's growing mental illness. Along the way, Kort doesn't pull any punches, and that's precisely why the novel is so powerful. By faithfully representing Laika's illness—by making it real on the page—Kort has crafted an important and sagely empathetic examination of mental illness' all too real human cost. At turns gritty and tender, *Laika* is a powerful and necessary novel."

—James Brubaker, author of *Liner Notes* and *Pilot Season*

laika

kate kort

Brick Mantel Books
Bloomington, Indiana

Published by Brick Mantel Books, USA

Brick Mantel
BOOKS

www.BrickMantelBooks.com
info@BrickMantelBooks.com

An imprint of Pen & Publish, Inc.
www.PenandPublish.com
Bloomington, Indiana
(314) 827-6567

Print ISBN: 978-1-941799-50-5
eBook ISBN: 978-1-941799-51-2

Library of Congress Control Number: 2017938486

Cover Design: Brent Smith

Printed on acid-free paper.

For Denny, who reminded me that manuscripts don't burn.

Acknowledgments

Thanks so much to everyone who helped this book come together. I'm grateful to Denny Young, whose sound advice and encouragement made *LAIKA* possible, and Lisa (Becker) Coad, for constant support, thoughtful edits, and hilarious wisdom. Thank you again to Jennifer Geist and Brick Mantel Books for welcoming a quirky experiment, and again to Brent Smith for designing a first-rate cover.

1

You walk quickly through the crowd going up Forty-Fourth Street. Once you're gone, you never look back. Never. You cross over Jackson Parkway, then cut through the alley west to your place on Matthias.

You're pretty sure he's on to you.

The back alley's deserted as you throw your backpack through the window and climb in after it. Everything's quiet except for your ragged breathing. You're thinking, *Should have taken Delaney this time, or at least doubled back through Brighton Hills.* You tack the scraps of black fabric back up on the window and collapse onto the milk crate that keeps you a couple of feet off the damp cement floor.

It's August and it's hot, but the basement air cools your sweat and slows your mind a bit. That one waiter was looking at you. You're sure of it now. He's there all the time, must work about fifty hours a week.

You think you've gotten good at sleight of hand, blending in, disappearing, but this time . . .

You jump off the crate and dump the contents of your backpack onto the dingy carpet remnant you've been sleeping on. A few slices of hard bread, half a baked potato, two pieces of cold boiled pork, and a golden apple, all wrapped in red cloth napkins. Not bad for three in the afternoon. But you can't really enjoy it now. You eat a slice of bread and carefully place everything else in the sectioned-off wine box in the corner of the room.

You stand up on the milk crate and slowly push back the makeshift curtains, scanning the gritty road. Nobody in sight. You'd know if someone had followed you.

Should have just gone the extra half mile to Delaney. You pick up the city map off the carpet and study it. You've spent weeks learning the streets, alleys, restaurants, markets, everything. It's hard to see the intersections anymore because you've scribbled over them so much, planning routes and detours and diversions in an endless effort to quell your fear. You wish your hair wasn't red—so noticeable against your pale skin. You might try to steal some dye. You could at least find some scissors and cut it. Maybe you'll do that.

Now you think maybe you should stop going to Yevgeny Alekseev's—that it's too dangerous. There are plenty of new places for you to try, but new places generally strip you of good sense and lock your heart in panic. You like low-risk, calculated, practiced.

But after this long, after starting to face the possibility that you screwed up and landed in the wrong city, you still can't stop looking for her.

You pull the crumpled photograph from your back pocket. Lena Nikolskaya Mishnev. You've seen it a thousand times, but still, you study it. A grainy snapshot of two little girls, both looking sullen and sitting on the front steps of their apartment in Novgorod, staring off past the camera. Their father, Kolya, took the picture and your mother, Anya, left it for you. Your dad said it was the only photograph she had of herself with her older sister from when they were young.

They eventually left and both settled in America, along the same coast, but you've only seen Lena once since your mother died. Your father gave you the photograph after a couple of years and you asked if you could visit her, but he acted offended and said he wasn't about to drive down five hours to see a near stranger who barely spoke English. But when you were eight your father finally told her she could come visit. She sat on your moldy couch with a glass of iced tea made from tea bags she'd brought herself and told you she'd be there if you needed her. Somehow it sounded harsh the way she said it, with her thick accent and terse speech, but she took your hand and looked you in the eye. She said your dad wasn't himself, that even after four years he needed more time to grieve and you just had to stay out of his way. You took the advice to heart, but eventually ran out of ways to be invisible.

So here you are, in the biggest city that's roughly five hours south of your home, the place with a promising Russian population, the block with the freshest Siberian tomatoes and Georgian cheese. The market that must be the best in the city.

You frown, bringing yourself back. The waiter noticed you. He was pretending to clear tables at the other side of the restaurant but he was watching. Once you met his gaze you got out of there, but it was probably too late. He'll remember you. He'll remember your long hair and your torn jeans. He'll remember your faded pink shirt and the scar over your eyebrow. He's probably put it together you're the girl who sometimes hides under the white baseball cap and broken sunglasses.

Or maybe he won't. Maybe he doesn't even care. Maybe he steals, too. Maybe he's got a lot of other things on his mind and what does he care if some kid takes a little food now and then? You decide not to worry about it because you've gotten pretty good at this and you're not going to make any more mistakes.

You lie down on the carpet and fall asleep because the black fabric that covers your only window blocks out all the light, and hardly anyone ever passes through the alley off Matthias.

> *Hey, did you see Ches in language arts this morning? He kept looking at you. Did you see when Mrs. Klein told him to focus and he got all red? Too bad he's such a dick. But if you like him I'll ask him out for you. I know you like Tommy, but sorry that shit's not happening. (I love you so I give it to you straight.) See you in Health. (Fuuuuck, I didn't do the reading . . . again.)*
>
> *BC*

You don't know why you keep the letters. You've got probably twenty of them in the bottom of your backpack, all folded into excruciatingly small triangles, and all from Britt. You feel bad, not saying goodbye to her. You hope she's not looking for you—that she's not hounding the police, telling them all your secrets and hoping they'll do something about it. You should have let her in on your plan, but it just seemed too risky.

You think about your friends, how they'll be starting high school soon. They must have forgotten you by now. Everyone except Britt. You think about the last time you talked to her—the day after that terrible night with the light bulb—when she wanted to know why you weren't at school. You composed yourself and told her you were sick and it was pretty gross so you probably couldn't go at all that week, but she saw through your bullshit and said you didn't sound sick. She said you sounded like something had happened. She said she could come over and "fuck shit up" if you wanted her to, but you laughed and said, "No, thanks." She always could make you laugh.

You read a few more letters, but they start to make you feel queasy so you fold them back up and put them away. You think about practicing your Russian but your mind's racing too much to focus. It's late and you find you don't have much left to give at the end of the day. You don't talk to people or follow a schedule or rush to meet deadlines, but it's still exhausting. You have to be invisible. You have to eat. You have to convince yourself you made the right decision. You have to force away enough darkness from your mind to allow you to get up each morning. But sometimes you can't. Sometimes you sleep all day and wish you'd never wake up.

2

Morning always catches you by surprise. Your watch says 10:37 a.m. and you think it's probably within an hour or so of being accurate, so you get up and eat one of the pieces of pork. *Saturday.* You sigh. You know it's easier to blend in, but you still hate how crowded the city is on the weekend.

Behind the decrepit furnace you find your hard plastic water bottle and pour some water into the lid. You splash it over your face and don't even bother to wipe it off. You pull out the mirror you took from the District Pharmacy eleven blocks away and glance at it uncertainly. Not as bad as you thought—you just look tired. Your eyes are hollow and watery, with no real color to them. Vaguely blue maybe, but more gray. Prison-gray. Dickens-gray. Suicide-gray.

You want to go to Yevgeny's but it wouldn't be smart. *Maybe Northside Diner instead.* No market, but plenty of outdoor seating and unobservant staff. And you could still pass Yevgeny's on the way.

You decide against the hat and just pull your hair back in a disheveled ponytail, then throw on your thin khakis and gray tank top, calculating it had been over a week since you appeared at the restaurant in that combination.

But it doesn't matter because he's not even there.

It seems your eagle-eyed waiter friend finally took a day off. *That's fine.* You just keep walking, glancing as you always do for Lena's face, more confident than ever in your decision to trek up to Northside. *Should never get stuck in a routine anyway.*

You hang out on the public bench across the street from the diner, pretending to read yesterday's paper. You wait for the large party to clear out. All older women. *Probably some bible study group or Mah-jongg club.* They're taking up about half the patio, so when they leave you've got to be quick before the waitress comes out to clear. It's not like it's stealing, though. They'll just throw it away.

You jump the small, decorative fence and mechanically go to work wrapping biscuits, fruit, sandwich remnants, anything, in napkins and sliding them into your backpack. None of the employees see, but a few customers are watching you. You don't worry about it, though; they always watch. They watch you and get this really sad look and start whispering to each other, but that's all they ever do. They never get you in trouble. They never help you.

You take the long way back, walking the side streets and cutting through the park, which you normally hate to do because you have to pass all the families, but not today. The weather's nice and you've got a few days' worth of food so you feel all right. You scan the ground as you walk, looking for loose change or anything discarded that could potentially be of use. You never know.

You hadn't believed it when you saw that busted cardboard box on the side of Forty-Ninth Street, completely full of old books. *The Fixer, Brave New World, Things Fall Apart.* They were too hard but you read them anyway, and you'll read the rest. You thought they were probably some kid's lit class rejects and you carried the box back with you, equal parts grateful to and infuriated by whomever dumped them there.

But you pass the familiar blocks leading to Matthias Avenue and understand not every day can be as lucky. A few cigarette butts, grimy trash, and newspapers are all you see. End of the line. You cut through the alley to the back of your warehouse, glance around, then slip in through the window.

You set out the food. Not bad, but most of it's perishable so you eat more than you usually would—fruit salad, half a BLT, some fried fish—and put the rest away. You almost feel full and it's unnerving. Like you've done something wrong.

You rifle through your box of books, but don't feel like starting anything new. Sometimes you wish there were a few easy Boxcar Children or Tom Quest books in there for you to read when you just want to relax. But you're in no position to make demands.

The old, tattered notebook catches your eye as you scan the warehouse. You don't want to write, you haven't for months, but you pick it up anyway.

There was a time when you drew a lot. The beginning of the journal has several sketches and pictures done in colored pencil or oil pastel that took you hours. They aren't great and they aren't creative—the earliest ones are mostly drawings of animals, then actors and musicians you liked—but you remember getting lost in them. You needed them.

You're now aware of a faint whine in your ears. Now that you're focused on it, you feel like it's been there since you got home. It's annoying and you look around for the source. You get up and walk by the furnace, the water heater, the steam pipes, but nothing's been working in the warehouse for a long time you guess, except the lights. *The lights.* You pull the cords and turn them off one by one until you're in darkness. You stand a minute, two minutes, breathing heavily. You think maybe it takes a while for the electricity to completely shut off, but after ten minutes you still hear the noise. Quickly, you pull the cords and bathe the room in light again. You don't want to think about it anymore.

You think about stealing money for a bus ticket. You've never done it before, actually robbed someone. The idea makes you sick, but you think about it anyway. Maybe you could take the money from restaurant tip jars or street musicians' cups. Maybe you could sell something—those books you found. Maybe you could beg. But whatever it is you do, the pull you feel, the drive to do it comes from that gnawing fear that's been eating at you for weeks: you're in the wrong place. There's no one here to help you. Your aunt is probably hundreds of miles away, if she even stayed in California, and just because your dad mentioned five hours and vaguely indicated south doesn't mean he had any idea what he was talking about. Maybe she's back in Novgorod. Maybe Kolya gave her the money to come back, if he's still alive. If any of them are still alive. You swallow against the knot in your throat and focus on your plan for tomorrow.

3

You walk by Yevgeny's the next day and casually pull an apple from the brimming basket in the outdoor market. You keep moving and don't look at anyone. You're not sticking around today. You head south on Lowry to Seventy-First and turn left. There's a farmer's market on Ames Avenue every other Wednesday and you think the heat will keep the crowd away this afternoon.

There's not much to look at on Seventy-First; it's a pretty desolate street with only a few open businesses and apartment complexes, but it's oddly crowded. You frown, periodically glancing up at the people walking by, trying to pick out details from their appearances to let you know why they're here. But every time you look up at them, they meet your eyes.

It startles you each time. *What do they want?* You've never had people on the street pay attention to you. Why would they?

But there it is again. You briefly dart your eyes toward a man in a business suit and he looks at you directly. Meaningfully. You shake your head. It's just your imagination. But you can't even lift your head without someone staring. Your face starts to flush but you feel cold and clammy. You stop in front of a reflective window to study your appearance but nothing seems off. *This is wrong.*

You turn to go back home. You thought you'd try a different place, out of your routine, in hopes of finding Lena, but there's something fucked up about Seventy-First and now all you want is to be back on your own shitty block.

"I'm leaving, all right?" you mutter to yourself, hoping to break the spell and send the onlookers back to wherever they belong.

You walk hurriedly now and don't look up at anyone, but they're not through with you yet. You start to hear them. They took that continual, soft hum in your head and turned it into low whispers. You frown and shake your head, but you're walking so fast it almost causes you to lose your balance. You take a breath and force yourself to slow down. You count to ten. More breaths. You look around. There are fewer people now, and no one's looking at you.

I just need more sleep. Some coffee. I need to get home.

You pass Douglass High School, their marquee advertising a back-to-school barbecue next week. You've bailed on your adventure for today, so maybe you'll try that. You just need some rest, that's all.

Things quiet down as you move back west. You turn on Jackson for a while, so you can get away from Seventy-First, then keep going down Forty-Ninth until you get to Matthias. You feel the apple in your backpack. At least you've got a good store of food and didn't need to go out today anyway. As usual though, a pang of guilt accompanies the satisfaction.

You think back to the first time you got in trouble for stealing. First grade. Your teacher kept bins of random toys in the classroom for everyone to play with at certain times of the day. There were marbles, beads, wooden shapes, plastic connectors, and coins. A bin of real coins to practice counting money. So one day you had a thought, kneeling there on the bright orange carpet, pretending to count change while the other kids built towers and strung beads. You knew you didn't have much money at home; your dad was always upset about the bills that came in the mail, the broken air conditioner, the doctor's visits and school supplies you needed. You put a nickel in your pocket, just to see what would happen. You went home and put it under your bed.

The next day you went to school and everything was normal. Nobody said a word about it. So you took a few more. It was a big bin and there were lots of coins, so it didn't seem to matter how many you took; there were always plenty left. After a few weeks you stopped taking the change, and decided to count what you had under your bed. Ten pennies, twenty-three nickels, sixteen dimes, and twelve quarters. You had never actually learned how to count money, so you weren't sure what their full amount was, but it seemed huge. You felt incredible. You had figured out a way to help and things would start to turn around.

You put the coins into one of your socks and held it for a moment, impressed by its weight. Then you carried it out into the kitchen where your dad sat, reading Belden's company handbook at the table. He was starting a new job, again.

"Hey," he said, looking up. "You're not hungry yet, are you?"

You shook your head, smiling. You set the sock down on the table.

"What've you got there?"

"Come see," you replied, still grinning like an idiot. You were so proud of yourself.

He got up and came around the table. He was already starting to frown but you ignored it. You were still good at ignoring things back then. He dumped the coins onto the table and you kept watching him as he stood there, as he tried to figure it out.

"Where did this come from?" he asked finally.

"Is it a lot? I knew it was a lot."

"Where did you get it?" His voice was low and controlled.

"From school." Your happiness was beginning to deflate. This wasn't at all like you had imagined it.

"They give you money at school?" he demanded.

You didn't want to tell him. If you had been a little older and a little smarter you might have come up with something fast, but it's hard for six-year-olds to switch gears when they run into trouble.

"It's from the toy bins," you mumbled. "We're supposed to count them. There are still a ton left," you added.

"You stole money from your classroom?" he shouted. "Are you fucking kidding me?"

Your eyes were fixed on his handbook so you wouldn't have to look at him and see how big your mistake was. But he didn't like that either. He hit you, probably to make you pay attention to him. It startled you and you cried, but he hit you again and you ran into your room.

You came out a couple of hours later because you were hungry. It might have been past dinnertime, you can't really remember, but when you got to the kitchen you saw the coins had been returned to the sock, which was waiting for you at your place. Your dad was still there, reading his handbook, but he was now accompanied by a bag of pretzels and a bottle of gin. He looked up.

"You'll put it back tomorrow," he said evenly. "Don't let anyone see you."

You nodded. Maybe he didn't need help after all. Maybe this job would be the one that stuck and things would start to get better. Maybe he'd start to forget about your mom. Maybe he'd start to like you.

You finally arrive at your warehouse on Matthias. You're happy to be home, and even though it's early you don't plan on going out again. You climb through the window.

You freeze. *Holy Jesus.*

It's a box.

There's a box sitting right in the middle of your floor and you have no idea where the fuck it came from.

You look around frantically. Someone's watching you. Someone's been in your place and now they're watching you.

Everything's quiet. You stand on the crate and look out the window but no one's there. You look at the box like it's a bomb. Maybe it is a bomb.

You start walking around the warehouse, silently. You're shaking again. You investigate the corners, go up in the crawl space, look behind empty crates and boxes stacked against the wall. There's nowhere else to hide. You check outside again, desperately searching for the slightest discrepancy in the alley's appearance. Nothing.

It's the police or the state or somebody. The more you think about it the more you believe it's true and your heart sinks. They're going to send you back.

Your eyes water and you glare at the box but decide if they're playing some game with you, then it's already over and you can just open the goddamn thing.

You walk over, sink down to your knees and pull back the cardboard flaps and look inside.

"What?" you murmur aloud to the empty room. You pull out a loaf of saran-wrapped banana bread and study it with distrustful curiosity. It looks homemade.

You slowly remove the contents of the box and set everything down around you on the floor. A Tupperware container filled with potato soup, an assortment of fresh fruits and vegetables, three bottles of water, and a jar of peanut butter. You laugh out loud but your heart's beating fast. The room gets a little darker and you grab for the empty box, clutching the sides. You throw up, coughing and sputtering, tears brimming in your eyes.

4

You don't leave your place for three days. You can't sleep because all you can think about is being found out. The food's a trick—some kind of trap—but you're not exactly sure how. You think of the people on the street, how they were all watching you with such interest. It could have been any one of them. You pack all your meager possessions into your backpack and keep it waiting by the milk crate in case you have to leave suddenly, for good.

On the fourth day, you start to hate yourself. You're so stupid. It makes you sick to think about the energy you waste keeping yourself alive. Maybe you deserve to be found out, to be sent back. *What does it matter? Can't keep this up forever.* Your chest burns as you start to think the lonely, desperate thoughts your mind works so hard to filter out, until you really scare yourself and decide you've spent too much time in this place and need to get out into the world.

1:24 p.m. You adjust your watch to the clock on the city bank building as you walk to Yevgeny Alekseev's.

In your mind you're already caught; in your mind you've got nothing left to lose so you forego the table scraps and go right to the adjoining market. You might as well have been a legitimate shopper, checking the produce for ripeness, reading the labels on packages of cheese, honey, and dried meat. You use the old trick of dropping a few apples to distract any bystanders from seeing you slip several items into your bag. You smile and pick them up, replacing them on the stand. With an unassuming expression, you make your way back around the sidewalk toward the front of the restaurant.

You know you're a fraud. You try to pretend nothing matters, and that gives you an occasional burst of confidence, but now your insides feel hollow and you wonder if you'll make it back to the warehouse. You shake your head disgustedly. *Pathetic.* And it's not like you needed it; you've still got plenty of food, but something scared you and told you to do it.

"Hi, there."

You jump, and barely stop yourself from crying out. You whirl around to see who spoke. It's him—the guy, the waiter. He's wiping down the windows. He smiles. Your face gets hot. He straightens up and looks like he'll say something else, but you turn back around and keep walking. You don't see where you're going; the streets and buildings blur together.

It's him. He's setting me up, making me lose my mind.

You stop and sit on a bench, no longer trusting your ability to walk, and run your hands feverishly over your face. *What does he want?* You can't be sure it's even him. Someone else could have left the box. You look back down the way you came. *Shit.* Now you have to leave. Even if it's not him it's somebody else and that means you're not safe anymore. It's okay; maybe you'll finally get to Lena. You'll try somewhere else. You've got to scrape up enough money for another bus ticket. You've got to find another abandoned warehouse. Steal another map and learn another city.

You go back to your place. You don't even empty out your bag to take inventory, but rather just toss it on the cement next to you. *It's him; I know it's him. Why can't he just leave me alone?* A heavy sigh escapes from your chest. He knows something. There's a plan coming together and you have to figure out what's going on or your next step won't even matter.

You fall asleep. It feels like that's all you ever do anymore.

5

The next day it's raining and you wake to the sound of water dripping onto the floor. It puddles up under the crate and slinks alongside the wall of the basement. 9:06 a.m. You move everything away from the sloping part of the cement floor and place your collection of food on top of a few empty boxes. The peanut butter jar catches your eye and you pull it off the box, unscrewing the cap and scooping out a mound of the smooth butter with your fingers.

You pick up your journal again, but you're even more jumbled and confused than before. You can't form your thoughts and you're afraid of what might come out if you start writing. You look up, your eyes moving toward your tower of boxes. There's a logo painted on the concrete wall, on the far side of the building by the back door. It says "Group 47" and was made using large, amateur stencils and green paint. You think the warehouse might have been some kind of unofficial meeting hall before it was completely abandoned. During your first few days here you glanced at that logo constantly. It bothered you. It felt intrusive. And it gave you a bad feeling, somehow. So you stacked boxes up against the wall until it was covered. This made you feel stupid, but there are so many things your mind needs to focus on, you couldn't let a dumb sign be one of them.

At 11:33 it stops raining. You snap your hair clip bookmark onto page sixty of *Dubliners* and reach for your backpack. The air outside is cool so you pull on your long-sleeved shirt and start the familiar walk toward Lowry Drive.

He's there, as usual, waiting on the scanty lunch crowd at Yevgeny Alekseev's. The view is pretty good from the bench at the corner of Lowry and Forty-Fourth, and you know he'd be hard pressed to spot you there. He's waiting on a table of three businessmen, taking drink orders. His smile turns your stomach. You dig out your book and pretend to read. *Average height. Looks about forty. Nice-looking, I guess; clean-cut.* One of the businessmen says something that gets the other two laughing, but your pal just keeps smiling politely. He doesn't make eye contact. *Seems nervous, awkward. Not too good with people.* You shake your head. *Nice career choice.* You stare at your book for a few minutes, watch the people walking up and down the street on their lunch breaks—try to appear interested in more than the Russian restaurant on the corner. But you aren't. He's back and every time you look at him you see something else. *No wedding ring. His shirt's wrinkled, tie's tied wrong. Probably lives alone.*

The longer you watch him the more you also realize he's a bad waiter. He's mixed up a few orders, dropped a tray, gotten yelled at. His voice is soft so you can never hear him when he speaks, but you doubt he's talking back. He looks up in your direction and you're paralyzed for a second, but he's looking past you at the loud college kids making their way across the street. You get up slowly, wiping your hands on your pants. You don't want to stay any longer.

6

That night you hear gunshots a few blocks away from your place. It doesn't take ten minutes before the sirens are so close they make your ears ring. You're wide-awake now and it feels like there's a rock in your stomach. *Wish I had a lock. At least I've got some good places to hide.* As you stand up to look around, your shaking legs force you back to the floor and you think you're going to cry. You didn't know it was like that. It's pretty clear the west side of town isn't exactly desirable, but somebody died tonight; you're sure of it. Somebody got killed in your neighborhood. You close your eyes but stay awake until morning. You *want* to want to go home.

The next day you spend hours studying your maps. You've walked probably hundreds of miles around the city and you know it pretty well. The west side is the only part of town where somebody can disappear like this. Where you won't be noticed. You look at the full state map and think about running to a new city.

You've got a Russian-language book and you practice a little every day, just in case. You don't remember how much English your aunt knows, but your dad always made it sound like she was an idiot for not assimilating better. He did his best to forget the little Russian he learned while your mom was alive, but you remember Lena spat a few angry phrases at him on her way out the door and you know he understood. You shake your head and move slightly away from a trickle of groundwater making its way across the floor. You still study her language but you know it's not looking good. You walk to the cardboard box that sits against the thick concrete wall opposite the window and pull out the book. You flip through its thin, water-damaged pages. *Sem'ya.* You toss it back in frustration. You still check the phone books everywhere you go, but in the back of your mind you know you're in the wrong goddamn place.

7

He's the only thing that forces you out of the warehouse the next day. It's after seven p.m. and you thought you'd stay inside for a few days at least, but you have too many questions. You need to know his agenda, why he wants to send you back.

"Graham!"

You look up from your book to see him walking swiftly out the back door of Yevgeny Alekseev's, trailed by another exasperated-looking waiter calling after him. You thought you'd do better behind the restaurant on the steps of the old library—you can only see about half of the back patio, but it's a much less obvious vantage point—and now here he is, maybe fifty feet from you, and there's no way out.

The other waiter grabs your guy's—Graham's—shoulder roughly to stop him.

"Hey, what is going on with you?" he shouts. "How goddamn hard can it—"

"Just back off, Jack," Graham interrupts. "Please. I'm taking a break."

Graham pulls out a cigarette and their voices lower to the point where you can no longer hear what they're saying. Jack still looks mad and Graham never takes his eyes off the ground as he agitatedly sucks on his cigarette. You have to try to slip away. If they even glance in your direction you'll be found out. The two seem engaged enough in their conversation for you to slowly rise to your feet and bring the straps of your backpack up over your shoulders. *Just be cool. They're not going to look.* They're talking a little louder now as you take a few painfully slow steps to the right. Jack yells at him to get his fucking act together, then storms back into the restaurant, leaving Graham alone to finish his cigarette. You're down the steps and onto the street by now, so you make the decision and keep walking without looking back, moving as silently as you can. You force yourself not to run, and head east to Delaney, then south to Fiftieth Street before you're confident enough to start toward Matthias.

But you're caught.

You feel tension on your backpack and automatically slip out of it and begin to run, but someone grabs your arm and forces you back. The world goes silent and it feels like you're drowning. Two months was all you could manage and now you're caught. You'll be put on a bus within the hour and you know exactly who will be waiting at the other end. They're probably calling him now.

You push blindly at whoever's holding you, but he gets your other arm and turns you around to face him.

"Hey, hey," Graham says calmly, frowning as you struggle to get away. "Hold on a minute, will you? Please; I'm not trying to hurt you."

You stop moving. It's startling to see him close up. His voice is still surprisingly soft, but his features are much more striking. He's not clean-shaven as you previously thought, but has a short layer of blond stubble covering his face, and his brown eyes are bloodshot and watery. *User,* you think automatically. *Booze probably. Maybe meth.*

You see he's watching you curiously, like he hasn't thought this through to his next move. *Whatever he wants, I guess he'll get it now,* you think despondently. *Maybe there's some kind of reward going for me.* The words barely make it through your mind before you start laughing at their absurdity. Graham looks at you apprehensively.

"Are you okay?"

You stop laughing but don't say anything. You remember what's happening.

"I just want to talk to you for a minute," he continues, leading you toward the bench at the corner of Fiftieth and Delaney. "I feel like I see you just about every day at the restaurant now," he says, letting go of your arm and sitting down. "Are you doing all right? I mean, do you need something?"

Run. It's a straight shot down Fiftieth. You look longingly down the street and are about halfway ready to take off, but you know he could catch you. He seems to know what you're thinking.

"Please," he says, indicating the bench. "Five minutes."

Reluctantly, you slide onto the bench next to him.

"My name's Graham," he begins. "Graham Calley. What's yours?"

Yeah, right. You glare at him until he turns away uncomfortably.

"Okay, well, I guess you know it was me who left the box of food." He glances toward you. "Is that why you've been watching me? 'Cause you know, if you need more—"

"Are you police?" you break in, unable to take it anymore.

"What? Police?" He's looking at you like you just called him a Nazi. "No, no. Why would you think I was police?"

"So what, then, State? Social services?" Your voice starts to waver and you hope he doesn't notice.

"What?" he asks, running a hand through his hair in bewilderment. "I don't understand. You know I work at the restaurant; why would you think I'm some kind of spy?"

"You're gonna turn me in."

"No."

You look at him carefully. His shirt looks worse today. It might not even be clean. His thin black tie is barely hanging together in its sad, inadequate knot, and his blond hair is so crazily unkempt you think he might have stuck a fork in a toaster back at work.

"What were you and that guy fighting about?" you ask. He suddenly makes eye contact and frowns. You've thrown him off.

"You mean Jack? At the restaurant?"

You nod.

Graham smiles slightly. "Jack thinks I'm in the wrong business. And he doesn't handle stress too well. He basically told me to get it together or quit."

"'Cause you're a shitty waiter?"

He laughs. "Something like that."

"Shouldn't you be there now?"

He shakes his head. "No."

You both sit in silence for a minute. You still think about running, but you have to know.

"What do you want?" you ask pointedly.

"What?"

"You said you wouldn't turn me in, so what's your angle?"

"I don't have an angle."

"Bullshit."

He sighs and gives you that sad look you hate. "I just thought you could use some help."

You laugh to yourself. *This guy thinks I'm just a dumb kid. I know what he's doing. Must be something in it for him.*

"How long have you been on your own?"

"Three years." You kick yourself immediately. It's not believable.

He smiles. "Three years? So, since you were, what, ten?"

"I'm eighteen." You can't drop your act now.

"Okay," he gives in, still smiling. "My mistake."

Laika

"How old are *you*?"

"Forty-one."

Silence again. You feel strange and wish you were alone.

"How long has it been?"

"How long has what been?"

"You said five minutes. What's it been?"

Graham looks around. "I don't know. You want to leave?"

You nod.

"Okay," he says, getting up. "Is there anything you need—"

You hold up your hand to stop him. "No," you say firmly. "I want you to stop with the food, okay? It's creepy. I want you to leave me alone."

He nods slowly. "Okay."

You've hurt his feelings but that just reminds you how much better he has it. Hurt feelings are a luxury—a problem that someone with a home and a job and food can afford to dwell on.

He rubs his forehead tiredly. "I'll see you around, okay?"

You reach for your bag cautiously, unsure if he's really going to let you go.

"No," you murmur, slipping it on. "You won't." You turn away from him and start running down Fiftieth without looking back.

8

Several days later you stand at your window. The evening is cooling off, and the sunset is brilliant on the horizon. You watch until the last embers of pink disappear into midnight blue, then you jump down off the milk crate and dig through your boxes of food one last time. *Gone. Again.* You've got a little peanut butter and a few carrots left. You turn all the boxes over again, throwing them aside and knowing you can't put it off anymore. *I've got to go back out. Tonight.*

A new place where you can look for your aunt. That'll put your mind at ease.

You don't like going any farther west than your own street for obvious reasons: the myriad drug dealers, shootings, prostitutes, the sad project housing, the passed-out homeless, and the faint sounds of children crying that serves as permanent white noise no one even notices anymore. But there's an untapped market there; no one knows you west of Matthias, and they sure as hell aren't going to notice you now. You've felt so unsafe these past few days, you told yourself you could wait. But now you need it. Tonight. You need the understaffed grocery stores and cafeteria-style restaurants—places where you can afford to make a mistake, get a little sloppy and not always pay the price. You don't feel like yourself. Or maybe you do, and that's the problem.

Harry's Grocery Outlet on Masarasky Road. *Why not? Looks as bad as any other place around here.* You walk through the automatic doors, scanning the patrons for Lena and trying to ignore the feeling that you've just picked this place out of a hat and there's no better chance of getting away with anything here than at Yevgeny Alekseev's.

Harry's is crowded, but no one matches her description. The dirty linoleum floor is covered in black marks from cheap shoes shuffling up and down the aisles. You pull your hat out of your backpack and put it on, hiding your face as much as you can. You come back outside and hang around the entrance, waiting for a family you can shadow. Thirty seconds later, there they are: a tall, bearded man of thirty-five or so, two boys, one who looks to be in high school and the other early middle school, and a girl of about seven. They have fair complexions and the ages seem to fit pretty well, so you start following them. They go a long way before putting anything in their cart, but the girl keeps pointing to things and asking, "Can we get that? Daddy, can we get that?" But the man doesn't say anything and they all just keep walking. You absently grab a jar of peanut butter off the shelf as you pass by. You want coffee, just the little tin of cheap instant, but they're going the other way.

Once you all get to the frozen food, the man starts putting several things into the cart. The kids watch as he tosses in chicken strips, piecrusts, French fries, ground hamburger, green beans, and peas.

"Pizza's on sale," the younger boy ventures. "Can we get one for this weekend? You know, when Mom's got another late shift?"

"No."

"But we never get to pick," he whines.

"Jeremy," his brother says sharply. "Shut up, all right?"

"No," Jeremy whines louder. *Shut up, Jeremy.* "Why can't we ever pick any—"

The man grabs Jeremy by the front of his shirt, ending the rest of his sentence.

"You earn the fucking money, you pick the food, all right?" the man growls.

The girl looks like she's going to cry and you turn around and run out of the store before you can hear any more.

You're almost to Prospect Avenue before you realize you're still holding the jar of peanut butter. *Goddamn Harry's.* You slip the jar into your backpack and slow to a walk.

It's getting late but you don't want to go back to the warehouse yet and you know you can't call it a night with just peanut butter. It's pathetic but you want something familiar. You're shaken and you're weak and tired and not thinking rationally and that's why you keep walking east toward Lowry Drive.

And, of course, things go wrong. You blame it on your weakness. You set out for Yevgeny's to make yourself feel better, but when you get close enough to smell the food, you realize it's not just the empty promise of your aunt that's been keeping you here. It's been weeks since you've tasted their rich blintzes or spicy shashlyks. Then you see all that food and forget to be clever.

The first rule you made for yourself with nice places like this was never go inside the restaurant. Outside seating lets you get in and out quickly, few if any surveillance cameras, no blocked exits. But you're edgy. You've had a crappy night and not much to show for it. You don't have the patience to wait for diners to clear out, and through the patio doors you can see somebody boxing up a to-go order. A big one. You walk around to the front entrance and wait until you see people heading in from the parking lot. *Let's try this again.* You slip in with a party of four and scan the restaurant quickly.

The to-go order is sitting on the counter. Just sitting there, waiting. Yevgeny's is smaller on the inside than you thought it would be. Very dimly lit, red and gold color scheme, ornately decorated. Mostly tables for two. Understaffed tonight. Glancing back at the counter, you see no one's around. *Do it, you fucking wuss. Do it now.* You decide, and you have to go. Now.

You walk over and pick up the bags like it's no big deal, then turn around to walk out the door. But you run right into him. Jack. You suppose he's coming to get that order. He smiles like he's going to apologize, then looks at the bags you're holding. He looks back at the counter and frowns, and you can't run away because he's blocking you and he's putting it together.

"Did you take those off the counter?" he asks in a low, hard voice. *Doesn't want to attract attention.*

You don't say anything.

"Come with me," Jack says, taking you by the arm and not giving you much of a choice. He leads you back behind the counter into the kitchen.

"You want to tell me what you're doing or do I have to call the cops?"

Your heart pounds but you look at him with the same blank expression and keep quiet. He grabs the bags out of your hands.

"You stealing from me?" His voice is getting loud.

You shake your head. *Calm him down; don't get him madder.*

"Then what in the hell—"

"Hey," Graham calls out, jogging in from the back patio. He smells like cigarette smoke. "What's going on here?" He looks at you worriedly, and his eyes harden as they move to Jack. "Jack, what are you doing?"

"This kid is stealing food!" he growls, shoving the bags into Graham's chest. "She practically had these out the door."

"Jack," he sighs in a patronizing tone, "this is my niece. Amy. She just came by while I was on break, and I asked her to run this order out so I could finish my cigarette."

Jack is still frowning. "Why didn't you just get me? I would have run it out. You can't have random kids acting like they work here."

"I know, Jack. I'm sorry. I just—you know how I am when I need a smoke; she just happened to be right there. And Amy, sorry I asked you to do that."

You nod. Jack looks at you carefully. You smile.

"Well," Jack sighs, "break's over now. Send her home and get back to work."

"Right."

Guess you'll have to call it a night after all. But now, even without food, getting to go back to your place is all you'd ever ask for.

9

Amy:

Hey, how's that for on-the-spot thinking? (My blood pressure is still through the roof, by the way.) Sorry if Jack scared you; he can be a little intense. Anyway, I thought you might be a bit surprised by this box. I know last time we talked you said no food, so I didn't include any. But seeing you the other night, I know you still need help. I've seen where you sleep and, as a father especially, it's been hard for me to think about. Sorry if this breaks the rules. I just want to help. No angle. By the way, I guess you're Amy until I know your real name. Hope that's okay.

Graham

In place of the moldy rug you've been sleeping on there now lie two medium-weight blankets, a light bed sheet and a comforter. You uneasily place your new pillow with its bright-white pillowcase in the middle of the bedding. *So he's a father.* The new setup makes the whole place feel different, but you can't really enjoy it. *Everybody's got something they want.*

You toss Graham's note aside. *Left this just two days after the thing with Jack,* you muse distrustfully. You feel like there's something you're not seeing—a part of his plan you should recognize. But as you flop down and lie flat on your new bed, you can't help smiling.

Usually you have no trouble falling asleep. Usually you think you're sleeping too much and you should try to set a schedule for yourself. But tonight you can't settle down. You're still on edge from getting caught by Jack. You're thinking about Graham. About Lena. About the family from Harry's and the people on Seventy-First and the coins from first grade and the logo on your wall. You're thinking about what your next move should be. You rarely have a solid plan, and even when you do, something always goes wrong.

After more than an hour of lying awake your mind starts to slow down. You close your eyes and wait to feel your body relax. But your hear something. Ticking. You sit up and look around, but you have no idea what could be ticking in the warehouse. *A bomb.* You look down. You hold your wrist up to your ear. It's your watch. You frown. *But it's digital.* Your digital watch is ticking. It doesn't make any sense but it's too late for you to try to figure it out so you take off your watch and shove it under a blanket. You eventually drift into an uneasy sleep.

10

Fucking hell. It's the little things that seem to thread their way through your brain, making it impossible to function. It's almost noon and the sun is maddeningly bright as you walk down Rushmore Boulevard. You forgot your sunglasses. You left your place with an idea, a mission of some kind, but along the way you forgot that, too.

Rushmore is full of the weekday lunch crowd. *Lunch.* You haven't eaten yet today. You haven't really thought about it. You study the shops and restaurants as you go by, but the only thing you can focus on are the people's reflections in the glass, drawing your attention back to the sidewalk. You feel watched. It's nothing new, but the feeling is amplified when the streets are busy. How many people have passed you? Fifty? Seventy-five? It only takes one. That hum in your head is now a buzz. You squint ahead. *Goddamn it.* A woman coming the other way slows her pace as you walk by, glancing in your direction. You speed up, shaking it off, but a man with two little kids does the same thing. They slow down. They look. Wheels begin to turn, setting in motion a machine much bigger than you are, and your breath is short. *I need to . . . I've got to get home, I just need—*

Someone grabs you and pulls you down. You're suddenly on your back, lying on the concrete and the sun is exploding your vision. You don't know what's happening, but you fight. You kick at the person pulling at your arm, shouting for him to back off.

"Hey!" you faintly hear, as if from a distance. "Hey, will you calm down?"

You stop kicking. It's a woman you don't recognize, maybe thirty, professional, serious.

"Why did you do that?" you sputter, sitting up. She looks at you oddly.

"You walked into traffic," she says. "I pulled you back onto the sidewalk." You look around to see several people staring. "You almost got hit," she continues, pointing to the intersection. There are tire marks on the road. You shake your head.

"Are you okay?" she asks, softening a bit.

"I just, I haven't eaten in a while and I, I forgot my sunglasses," you begin, running your hand over your eyes. "I kept seeing these people, you know, on the street . . ."

You look up to see this woman is watching you carefully and you stop talking. You forgot where you were. Where you need to be.

"I'm sorry; I'm fine. I have to go. Thank you . . . for that," you say, gesturing toward the street. You get up and awkwardly make your way back up Rushmore before she can say anything else.

Chapter 11

Graham

Pain Is in the Resistance

He didn't want to tell Schwartz he'd been up all night. He didn't want that to be the focus. Schwartz always seemed to know, though, and Graham wasn't sure how to conceal it.

"Hey," he said, smiling as Graham walked into his office, "you're early."

"Sorry." Graham glanced at the clock on the wall, but the numbers looked small and blurry. "Should I wait out there?"

"No, no." Schwartz rose from his chair and walked around his desk. "Let's get started."

Dr. Schwartz was about sixty-five, with gray and black corkscrews of hair and a thick mustache. Graham liked him, but always got the feeling he kept a lot to himself—that he wrote the things that were too terrible to say on his legal tablet, for his own future use.

"Your eyes are red," Schwartz remarked. He sat in his reading chair and adjusted his glasses, the ones he wore on days when he'd forget to put in his corrective lenses. He narrowed his gaze at Graham. "Late night?"

"I guess."

"All night?"

"Listen," Graham said quickly, "something's been on my mind I think I should tell you about."

"All right."

Graham looked around the office—its drab, gray paint and dim lighting. Neutral artwork that practically faded into the walls. There was a new bookshelf—an impressive floor-to-ceiling piece made of dark wood with carved details. Schwartz must be doing all right. Graham avoided his eyes, trying to decide what to say. Wanting it to come out right.

"There's this girl—a runaway, I'm sure—who's been coming by the restaurant. I've been trying to help her out with food and that kind of thing, but I get the feeling she's not well."

"What do you mean?"

"I don't know. I think she might have some kind of autism. Some of her behaviors and mannerisms are similar to Emerson's. I just, I really feel like I should be doing more to help her."

The streetlight outside the window flickered on, then back off, and Graham frowned. The window was always uncovered during his sessions, but there was a rolled-up blackout shade at the top and thick burgundy curtains pushed off to the sides. He wondered why Schwartz would need to make it that dark. And why he'd never thought about it before.

"And she reminds you of Emerson?"

"What?"

"The girl—she reminds you of Emerson?"

"Somewhat, I guess."

"Is that why you want to help her?"

"I want to help her because she's in trouble." Graham looked down and began pulling tensely at a thread on his jeans. Maybe this was the wrong time. Maybe Schwartz just wouldn't understand.

"A lot of people are in trouble. It's a big city, with a huge homeless population."

"You think I should just forget it?"

"No," Schwartz smiled, "I'm just interested in why this girl in particular has been on your mind."

"She just comes around a lot."

Graham heard voices in the hall and knew the guy who saw Dr. Cain next door had just arrived. Always late.

"Do you talk to her?"

"What?"

"The girl. Do you talk to her?"

"A little. But it makes her nervous."

"I'd imagine," Schwartz said, reaching for his notepad. "If she's in trouble, though, you should probably get the police involved."

"Right." Graham nodded, but Schwartz was missing the point and getting him frustrated, so he just wanted to drop it.

"Is that why you didn't sleep last night?"

He smiled a little, thinking back to the night before, even though it wasn't funny at all.

"No. Something else happened."

"What?"

"I was walking home down Forty-Second over by Delaney—"

"This was last night?" Schwartz broke in.

"That's right."

"So you were walking home from a meeting?"

"Yeah."

"Okay. Sorry; go on."

"Well, I was getting ready to cut through the park when I passed some guys smoking on the corner. They called out to me and said not to forget my bag."

Graham closed his eyes, his heartbeat quickening. When he opened them, Schwartz was writing.

"Your bag?"

"Yeah, they had a backpack with them. When one of the guys handed it to me I saw it was full of drugs. Maybe cocaine or heroin, I don't know. I kept telling them it wasn't my shit and they should get it out of there, but they wouldn't listen. They were sure they'd talked to me before. They said they'd been waiting for me and it was hell getting the drugs that fast and they don't usually rush it for new people so I'd better turn into a loyal customer."

Schwartz nodded but didn't say anything.

"But then, a group of people walked by and the guys turned away, you know, trying to act natural, so I slipped into the group and when I got to the park I just ran."

"You ran all the way home?"

"No, I had to stop when I got to Prospect. My lungs couldn't take it."

"But then you couldn't sleep."

"Yeah."

"Because these guys scared you."

"Yeah." Graham frowned.

"Was it more than that?"

"I don't know. I mean, they thought I was a junkie." Schwartz nodded. "And I know it's stupid, but part of me wanted to track them down and tell them what I've been through and how it took me years to reconstruct my life, and I'd never throw it away like that."

"Do you think that would have made you feel better?"

"Yes."

"And you really would have told them, if you'd had the chance?"

"I think so."

Schwartz laughed. "Graham, I can't pay you to talk about the accident with me. Every time I lead you in that direction, you evade my questions or change the subject or just refuse to talk about it. But you would have done it with these guys?"

Graham shrugged, pulling at the thread again. "I'd never see them again."

"You'll never see them again as it is, and yet their impression of you still matters. It kept you up all night."

"Sometimes I feel like I want to justify myself to people. You know, give them an explanation for why I forget things, or start shaking all of a sudden, or look like a drug addict."

"Maybe you also feel the need to get this story off your chest sometimes."

"I guess that's part of it."

"Can I ask you something else?" Schwartz shifted in his chair.

"Sure."

"Do you feel you have to justify your survival?"

"What do you mean?" he asked warily.

"You want to apologize for the way you are now, even to total strangers." Schwartz was watching him with concern. "You once told me you felt you should have died that day in Germany. Do you feel an impulse to justify why you're still here?"

Graham sighed and leaned back in his chair. "I just wanted a break from talking about it here."

"Okay. But it's been four months."

"I know."

"Your insomnia's getting worse again," Schwartz reminded him, writing on his pad. "Your thoughts seem scattered, and I know this is directly related to the issues you haven't let us address."

"I have plenty of issues we get to address." Graham forced a smile so Schwartz would see he was trying to make a joke.

"It's true," he replied. "Every time you come in you have a new story to tell me, like you're trying to keep me busy. Like you're trying to fill this hour with anything but the real problem."

"You don't think they're important?" Graham asked, frowning again. "You don't think this girl at the restaurant is important?"

"Of course I do," Schwartz replied calmly. "But there's an order to things." He set down his legal tablet and leaned forward, resting his forearms on his knees. "Let's say you start helping this girl, right now, using your position at the restaurant to provide her food, and you also give her a bit of money, all right?"

"Okay."

"Meanwhile your insomnia continues. You're overtired and you start slipping up at work, dropping things, forgetting things. Your stress level increases because Jack's yelling at you and threatening your job. Your nightmares get worse; maybe your hallucinations come back. You're unable to function and you get fired from the restaurant. You've got nothing now. So the girl is back to stealing and begging, and you have to start over again."

Graham sat silently for a moment. "You paint quite a picture," he finally mumbled.

"I'm not saying any of that will happen," Schwartz explained, "but you have to know nothing will get better until you address the accident. With me," he added, "not some guys on the street."

Graham looked up at the clock again, hoping it would be nearly time to leave, but half the session still remained.

"Can I take a break?" he asked, standing up and indicating the door. "Just for a minute?"

"Absolutely."

Graham walked out the door of the medical building and was hit by the sticky, salty air. He pulled out his cigarettes and leaned his back against a payphone booth, striking a match but letting it burn a moment, watching the flame recede, before holding it to the end of the cigarette. It was a quarter till seven, and he wondered if Emerson had left for her play rehearsal yet. If maybe he could call and hear her voice.

Graham moved into the booth and slid a quarter into the slot. Six rings before Anna picked up. *Barry must be over.*

"Hello?"

"Hey, Anna."

"Graham, what's up?" she asked, sounding relaxed.

"Not much. Is Emerson still there?"

"No, she left about ten minutes ago. She got a ride with her friend, Jani. Sorry," she added.

"That's all right." He rubbed his eyes. "So, I guess Bobby's coming over, then?"

"Shut up," Anna laughed. "Your shtick is getting old." She paused. "And yes, he's here."

"Well, I should let you go. I've got to get back in there anyway."

"Are you at work?"

"Therapy."

"How's it going?"

"I guess I'm pulling my same old shit," he laughed. "He thinks I'm wasting our time."

"Are you?"

"I don't think so."

"Well, it's your money, Graham," she said firmly. "If it's helping you, that's all that matters."

"Yeah."

"How have you been sleeping?"

"Fine."

"Really?"

"Yeah. I'm sorry," he said quickly, "I really should get back."

"All right. I guess I should relieve Barry." She sighed. "He's looking over this work contract for me."

"Well, just make sure he bills you the family rate."

"I'll have Emerson call you first thing tomorrow," she said, her voice betraying her smile.

"Thanks. Good night."

12

You still spy on him. He always seems to know when you're there, though, and it still stops your heart to meet his gaze, no matter how often it happens. *Could be some sicko—a pervert or something,* you think as you walk away. *But he had me alone and didn't try anything. Could be trying to build trust, though; could be waiting for me to like him, feel sorry for him, think he's different.*

You know you should tell him off for good and get him to stop coming around. It doesn't sit well with you that he knows where you live. A potential serial killer. But you're getting help, and you have to admit that's nice.

> *Hey, Amy:*
>
> *So my sister gave me some hand-me-downs the other day, which I usually put in storage for my daughter, but my niece is just a few years older than you, I think. I hope there's stuff in here you like/can use. It seems she was especially into teen boy bands, so that should explain a lot of the t-shirts. Could always be pajamas, I guess.*
>
> *Graham*

Most of the stuff actually fits, you think. The jeans are a little big, but in much better shape than anything you've had before. You pull out everything you can use. Style doesn't matter, just the size. The solid-colored shirts will be best in terms of blending in, but you think maybe you'll take Graham's advice and use the others as pajamas. It's nice and it's useful but you're still overwhelmed. He's going out of his way and you're not sure what to think.

That night you start writing again. You only have twenty or thirty blank pages left in your journal. The rest is filled with entries, story ideas, dreams, and nightmares, all scrawled out in horrendous handwriting. You always worried about keeping it around back home. A few times you thought about destroying it; it wasn't safe. But now you're gone and if he finds the journal it means he finds you and that means you've got a lot more to worry about than some stupid writing that means nothing.

You pull the cord from the ceiling that illuminates a bare bulb. You turn to one of the blank pages and crease it along the book's binding. You pick up the pen and jolt back there. Back then.

> *It was almost two in the morning. I couldn't sleep I was so fucked up. And I kept seeing light every time I moved my eyes. Like a zing or a jolt from the corners. I smacked my head to try and make it go away, but that just made a bigger burst, like fireworks. And it killed. This time was one of the worst. Maybe the worst. I looked like I was dying until I washed all the blood away. And my rib—left side, third from the top—never did heal right.*

You stop. You don't know why you're writing this. To turn in to the police? To hold onto until he finds you and wants to bring you back? To prove to yourself ten years down the line that it all actually happened when you try to tell yourself you're normal and everything's always been fine? You look around at your clothes and your blankets and sigh discontentedly. *What is Graham doing?*

You blow the hair off your forehead. *Fuck it.*

> *The bed was hot so I got up and stood by the window. School would be out soon, and then there would be nowhere to go. Summer. I wished I was old enough to get a job but I wasn't old enough for anything. It didn't matter, though, because I was leaving. Then I heard a creak in the floor and froze. I waited a minute, five minutes, letting those sparks shoot across my eyes, but I didn't hear anything else. I felt crazy. I knew he had passed out. It had to have been the dog, but I couldn't stop shaking. I thought about that night, and what I had done. The light bulb.*

You inadvertently squint up at the light bulb above your head. *I don't want to do this anymore.* You put away the notebook—shove it under a few boxes in the corner—and turn off the light, lying down in the darkness.

13

What the hell am I doing here?

There are people everywhere. It's your brilliant plan—the Douglass High School barbecue—but now you feel like it might be better to starve than be around all these students. There are just so many of them, talking and laughing and acting bizarre, and you didn't think it would be so overwhelming because you're the outsider but it feels like somehow they're all making fun of you.

The sun beats down as you make your way over to the tables of food. *I'll just grab what I can and go. This is too many people.* You take a paper plate and shakily pile it with hamburger patties, slices of American cheese, buns, baby carrots, and barbecue potato chips. With one hand resting on top of the food mountain in an attempt to steady it, you weave through groups of friends with your eyes lowered, heart pounding.

"Whoa, is that all for you?" a small voice asks with genuine admiration. You look up to see a girl, your age maybe, with a red headband and a slight Spanish accent.

"Yeah," you whisper, feeling the sweat make its way to the surface of your skin.

"You must have some crazy metabolism," she says, smiling.

You manage a laugh but don't say anything. You take a step away but the girl doesn't seem to notice.

"What grade are you going into?"

You look up at the school, remembering where you are. "Ninth."

"Me, too," she says happily. "Who's your homeroom teacher?"

"Uh, well," you stammer, trying hard not to drop your plate of food, "I, actually, I can't remember his name."

"But it's a guy? Then it has to be either Mr. Crane or Mr. Schneider. I've got Mrs. Cole. I know she's supposed to be really strict and everything, but my brother had her last year and said she's fine as long as you actually pay attention and don't skip a lot of class and that kind of thing."

You nod and get ready to make an excuse to leave, but she's taken a breath and is talking again.

"I'm Kyrie, by the way. Kyrie Salazar. But if you went to Douglass Middle you already know my brother, Eli."

You shake your head.

"Well, I guarantee you'll know him within the first week of school here. He's got one of those magnetic personalities, you know? Like Ferris Bueller. I mean, everyone knows him. It's pretty annoying sometimes, but he's a good guy, and he's amazing at math if you ever need help with your homework."

Your head feels cloudy and you think maybe you don't need an excuse to leave because you'll just pass out in a minute or so and that'll take care of it. You can tell by her tone and face and body language that Kyrie has no idea how uncomfortable you are, and it'll take a fairly strong hint to get her there. You look around nervously. More people keep showing up. *More adults.*

"Hey, let's sit down so you can eat," Kyrie is saying, already leading you to an empty section at one of the long banquet tables. You both sit down and you realize just how intimidated you are by this friendly girl in the red headband. For some reason it would kill you to be rude to her. "So what's your name?" she asks, watching you intently as you piece together your first cheeseburger.

"Amy," you say, with the first hint of a smile you've had all day. "I'm kind of new to the area."

"Hey, I know what that's like," Kyrie says with a laugh. "When I was six my family moved here from Chile. My dad works in banking and finances and they offered him a really good job. And my mom writes for this magazine, so she can do that wherever we live." She pauses. "Where did you move from?"

"Oh, just a little ways up north," you say vaguely.

She nods and, to your relief, changes the subject. "Yeah, it's nice around here; I like it a lot. You know, I could show you around sometime if you want. I know the area pretty well, and there's a lot to do if you know where to look."

To this you have no response; you just stare at her quizzically, wondering what could possibly make a person so welcoming and trusting of ragged strangers. Again, she is oblivious to your hesitance. In fact, she's already moving on.

"So what's your schedule like? I'm really excited to study literature. I love English classes, and Spanish classes, too; someday I want to be a writer or a journalist or use something with language. Maybe a linguist. I think that would be so much fun. But I can't take those kinds of classes until later. Kind of a drag, but I really like my schedule for this year, so I guess I don't really care."

"You like to read?" you ask, proud of yourself for coming up with something to say.

"Oh, yes," Kyrie replies with a smile, letting you know your question was an understatement. "It's probably my favorite thing to do." She looks around the school lawn for a moment, her dreamy expression fading slowly. "Are you here by yourself?"

You jump a little. The question sounds very harsh for some reason. You nod cautiously.

"So your parents work a lot, too?" she asks with a sympathetic smile.

"Yeah. All the time." You decide it's time to get out before Kyrie starts with all the family questions. "I've actually got to go. I told my little brother I'd bring him home some food from this thing, so . . ." You gesture toward the still massive plate of food and pick it up carefully. "But I guess I'll see you around?"

"Definitely," she replies. "I should probably find Dave anyway; he's my brother's friend who gave us a ride." She rises to her feet then stops. "Hey, there's this new bookstore opening on Freelander Boulevard. Maybe we could check it out one day after school. It's supposed to be pretty cool."

I've never been that far east. "Yeah. Sounds fun."

"Great. See you Monday."

Kyrie waves and you turn around and make your way back through the throng of people to the street. *See you Monday.*

14

You wake up on Monday and think about Kyrie and Eli and Dave walking to school. You picture them carrying backpacks and lunches and talking about their new homeroom teachers, nervous about their new classes and making new friends but ready to begin after a long, uneventful summer. You see them running in the rain, laughing and holding their backpacks over their heads. *No, they probably have raincoats with hoods.* You see Kyrie reading in the back of her math class when the teacher's not looking; you see her befriending another new freshman whose locker is right next to hers and pushing Eli playfully as he passes by; you see she's already forgotten you.

Just as well, you think as you get dressed and splash some water on your face. *How long would it have taken her to figure out I was a fake? A day maybe?* You get ready to leave, but as you climb out the window you see something lying off to the side. It's another box, damp from the rain. You pull it inside and sit on the milk crate. It's small, a shoebox, and not very heavy. You open the lid and find a note:

> *Hey, Ames (see how I get creative?):*
>
> *If you can, come by the restaurant tonight at closing. I'll be the last one there and I can send you home with all the leftover food. And the books are just because I know you like to read. These are a couple of my favorites. See you (hopefully) tonight.*
>
> *Graham*

You pull three books out of the box: *Leaves of Grass, Lilies of the Field,* and *Mrs. Frisby and the Rats of NIMH.* You crumple the note. *Not today, rapist.*

You don't go near Yevgeny's all day. You don't go anywhere in particular, but end up at the city park. You sit on the bench with your book and your broken sunglasses and try to feel like you're taking a break from your life. You don't scan the area for forgotten belongings. You don't obsessively monitor the people to make sure no one's interested in you. You don't look for him in every father on the playground. But it doesn't last. It's not a safe way to live. You think about what he's probably doing to find you. How it's only a matter of time. You think about Graham and his forwardness, his insistence, his motives.

On the way home you stop by Jackson Parkway Sporting Goods and steal a pocketknife. It's time you got smart.

15

You don't want to write tonight. Instead, you flip to the middle of your journal and start to read. You smile. There are things you really do miss.

9/93

Britt says I have hair like a movie star and I'll probably get a boyfriend this year. She doesn't want another boyfriend, though. She says after they get what they want they break up with you.

You never did get a boyfriend that year. But you weren't that interested anyway. Britt filled up most of your free time with trips to the shopping center and hikes through the woods that surrounded your neighborhood. And you filled hers with endless games of truth-or-dare and midnight bonfires at your cousin's house. She was the visionary and you were the smart-ass. She was the only one who had any idea what was going on. You flip through.

5/94

I was supposed to go camping with Britt's family this weekend. I was all packed and everything, but of course it didn't happen. When Dad got home I asked him if he could drop me off at her house and he lost it. He yelled and acted like it was coming out of nowhere. He didn't remember saying yes. He always does that. I was mad so I told him he was wrong—that he already told me I could go. He called me a liar and hit me. And then I got belted. Because I tried to go camping with my friend.

Your eyes sting as you go back several pages. You read a few lines and your heart beats fast. You don't remember this one right away. The date says you were ten.

10/91

Dad talked about Mom today. It was so weird. He was helping me with my homework, and then just stopped. He looked really tired. He told me to come sit on the couch with him and brought out a couple pictures to show me. He said he doesn't want me to forget her. But I was only four. I feel bad, but I already have.

He showed me their wedding photo, and one of them at an amusement park. He showed me one of her as a little girl in Novgorod. She was sitting with a kitten on her lap. Then he laughed and it startled me. He told me she took care of all the strays in her neighborhood.

I didn't know what to say so I just looked at the pictures until Dad got up. Before he went in to bed he kissed my head. I can't remember him ever doing that before.

You look up because there's rustling outside your window. You wipe your eyes and pull the knife out of your pocket. It's 12:17 a.m. You turn out the light and back slowly into the corner of the room, potential fight-or-flight scenarios running through your head. You hear glass break and a murmur of "damn it" outside the window. You frown. It's Graham. You think about hiding until he's gone, but you can't let him leave. You can't let it keep happening. So you turn on the light and uncover the window.

Chapter 16

Graham

More Will Be Revealed

"Hey," Graham muttered without looking up, shaking his head in annoyance. He picked up the shards of glass from the pavement beside the box he'd brought. "I was just going to leave this . . . damn it."

He wished he could have done just this one thing right, but he hadn't slept the past two nights and that made his hands shaky and his balance off. He'd been dropping things at work, too, as Jack reminded him. Graham looked up and "Amy" was eyeing him distrustfully. Her long, red hair wasn't pulled back this time and its color was striking as it spilled over her shoulders. She was wearing some of the clothes he'd brought her, which gave him back a shred of confidence in whatever it was he was doing. She climbed out of the window.

"What are you doing here?"

"When you didn't come by tonight, I wanted to make sure you got the food." Graham paused. "Why didn't you come by?"

She was glaring at him now. He wanted to leave, to go home and try to get a few hours of sleep before daylight came to mock him again. Emerson would be over tomorrow and he didn't want to be a zombie for her. But Amy needed help.

"Okay, let's see," she began in an abrasive, snarky tone Graham was sure he could expect from Emerson in a few years. "You tell me to meet you at the restaurant after dark when you're the only one there. You know I have no one looking out for me." She leaned against the building. "You have a kid, right? A girl? Would you want her doing that?"

Graham started to feel sick. This was how he came off to people. A junkie. A rapist. A lowlife.

"No," he said slowly. "No. I didn't mean to come off that way. That's not what I meant at all."

"Will you stop, then? Just stop with all of it, all right?"

She was getting worked up and his stomach was sinking. He'd scared her, and made things worse again. He wanted to tell her she could trust him, that he did have a daughter and he'd do anything for her, and that he'd do the same . . . but it all sounded perverted when he ran it through her lens.

"Amy, listen—"

"My name's not Amy." Her voice was flat. "And I don't know what you want but you're just making it harder, okay? If you come by again, I'm leaving. I've learned the city pretty well and I can find a new place."

Graham frowned and took a step forward, intending to apologize, but she held up her hands to keep him back. He stopped.

"Is that a knife?"

She glanced at it. "It's a dangerous city."

His heartbeat picked up. *She might use it.* "Okay. You're right." Graham thought about what her past must be like—why she's running. *Maybe an orphan; a ward of the state.* "I won't come back. I promise."

She didn't say anything. He saw she was shaking slightly, the knife still clenched in her hand.

"Okay, well . . ." Graham rubbed his eyes, still flustered. "Take care of yourself, all right?"

She nodded. "Good night."

He turned back the way he came, but didn't feel right leaving things that way. He looked over his shoulder but she was already back inside the warehouse, and the box was gone. But he'd back off. He wouldn't come around anymore because there's nothing worse than thinking someone's out to get you.

"I'm going to the bathroom, okay?" Emerson eyed her father warily. "Don't cheat."

Graham held his hands up and scooted his chair back, away from the game board on the kitchen table.

"Hey, I only cheat when we're into the third hour."

She narrowed her eyes. "I know where everything is."

He stood up to fill his water glass, and glanced at the clock over the microwave. It was nearly nine and Emerson didn't seem tired at all. Anna said she'd pushed her bedtime back to nine-thirty because she hadn't been able to fall asleep any earlier lately.

"Would it make you feel better if I step out for a minute?" he asked, turning back to her. "So you'll know for sure I didn't cheat?"

She smiled slightly and ultimately nodded.

"Okay. I'll meet you back here in a minute."

Emerson turned toward the hallway and Graham slipped out the front door. He jogged down the stairs and out the entry of the apartment complex, hoping to get a quick smoke in. He pulled his cigarettes out of his back jeans pocket along with the orange matchbook from Julian's, a restaurant down the street. He drew a match from the book and held it against the strike strip, but felt himself hesitate. He frowned. *Don't be weak.* Graham steadied himself, holding his index finger resignedly against the head of the match and tried again to force it across, but his hands were beginning to shake and sweat started to burn under his arms. He looked at the cigarettes in one hand, one already freed from the pack and resting between his fingers, and the useless matches in the other.

"Fuck!" he snarled under his breath, crumpling the cigarettes in his hand. He stuffed everything back into his pockets and sat on the first step of the complex, waiting for his heart rate to slow down.

Graham hadn't thought much of it a few months ago, when Dr. Schwartz told him to get rid of his lighter and start carrying real matches. He'd said it was a way to start gaining back a comfort level with fire. Lighters were too controlled, too predictable, he'd told him. So Graham agreed and didn't give it much thought until a few weeks later when he lit a match and then froze, paralyzed with fear. He'd watched as the flame crept closer and closer to his fingers, unable to think or move or do anything to stop it. The burning heat finally broke his trance as it singed his thumb and he dropped the match, stomping it into dust and leaving a black smudge on the concrete behind Yevgeny's. It was a pathetic, sickening feeling that followed, one that only confirmed Graham's belief in his inability to function in the real world, even after all he'd overcome.

Emerson was back at the table when he walked into the apartment. Her face was blank and her eyes looked vacant, so Graham thought she might have been more tired than she'd let on. She looked up at him.

"You were outside." Her voice was monotone, which it got sometimes, and he knew she'd start to pull away soon.

"Yes," he said, sitting back down. "I wanted to get some air."

She studied him. "But you didn't smoke."

Graham smiled slightly, feeling a pang of guilt to remember she was aware of his addiction. "How do you know?"

"I don't smell it."

"No. Just wanted some air."

She idly scratched her Monopoly token against the top of the table. The iron. She always picked the iron. She was avoiding his eyes.

"Should we finish this tomorrow?" he asked gently. "You can still have some time to play in your room before bed."

"By myself?" she asked, looking up.

Graham nodded. She seemed relieved and stood up, placing her iron back on the board. He told her good night and she indulged him in a high-five before heading off to her room.

He sat alone in the kitchen for several minutes, thinking. He considered calling Anna, but it was nothing they hadn't talked about before. Talked about with doctors. Emerson's desire to be alone, her voice that sometimes lost its emotion, her aversion to touch and eye contact. Graham sighed and rubbed his eyes. It was relatively mild, they'd said, but the signs pointed to autism. He thought again of Amy.

Most days, Graham determined, he thought about Amy every hour or two. More often when he was at the restaurant. He knew she was alone, young (maybe thirteen or fourteen), fairly new to the city, and exceedingly distrustful. Sometimes he thought he should call the police, but a feeling nagged at him and prevented him from doing it. He didn't know her story. He only knew she needed help, and would push it away in the same manner his own daughter would, right at the time when it would matter the most.

Graham rose from the table, leaving the game board intact. He threw away a few Chick-O-Stick wrappers and put a six-pack of Coke in the fridge. He glanced at the slip of paper held with a pineapple-shaped magnet to the top left corner of the fridge. He ran his fingers over the red ink. "90–90." He closed his eyes. Then he switched off the lights and turned down the hall to his bedroom, hoping to read awhile and finally get some sleep.

Graham yelled and grabbed for the man next to him, the one who had been idly reading a copy of *Frankfurter Neue Presse*, but it was only a rumpled pillow that came back in his shaky hands. He ripped off his shirt and touched his stomach, but the metal he'd felt stabbing him only a moment before was gone. He lay back, choking on his hoarse breath. He waited a minute. Ten minutes. He couldn't get his pulse back to normal. He couldn't keep doing this. He turned to the digital clock on his nightstand. 4:15. He rubbed his face. *It's over.*

He got out of bed and stumbled to the kitchen. He lifted the phone off its cradle on the wall and punched in Anna's number. He got the intercept message, though, telling him his call couldn't be completed. He checked the fridge,

90–90

reading the note with her new number on it, and tried again, steadying his hands as best he could while he dialed. It rang. Graham collapsed into a chair and listened, his leg jittering. Seven rings before it went to the machine. He hung up and dialed again. Seven rings, machine. *She's at Barry's.* He slammed the phone back onto the wall, forgetting Emerson was asleep down the hall.

He paced the kitchen feverishly, muttering to himself. His heart was still racing and his shirt was damp with sweat. He was glad he didn't have Barry's number, because he knew he'd call it. Graham could just imagine what Barry would say to Anna after their conversation. *Graham, again? He can't just call you in the middle of the night, ranting like a lunatic whenever he wants. Anna,* he would say, patronizingly, in his best law professor voice, *do you really trust this man with your daughter? What if he's hallucinating again? What if it's even worse?*

Graham stopped. He pushed aside a few papers on the small desk under the phone until he found the one he wanted. He hesitated for only a moment before picking up the phone again.

Walt answered on the third ring.

"Walt Morgan," he said groggily, in the well-rehearsed manner of a seasoned businessman.

"I'm sorry, Walt," Graham began, immediately regretting his decision. "I'm sorry it's so early."

"No, Graham. No, it's fine," he answered quickly. "What's up?"

"I don't know." He rubbed his eyes. "I had another nightmare. They're getting worse again."

"I'm sorry."

"Yeah."

"Did you break anything?"

"No." Graham sat at the kitchen table. "I called Anna, but I think she's at Barry's."

"You feel like you need me there?"

"No." He paused. "I'm sorry, I shouldn't have called you."

"No, Graham," Walt said firmly, "I'm your friend, too. I'm glad you're not in that place." He coughed a few times. "I can still come over, if you want."

"No. No, you don't have to do that," he sighed. "I appreciate it, but I think I just needed to hear someone else's voice. I get so detached sometimes . . . I don't know what to do."

"Is Emerson there?"

"Yeah. She's asleep."

"Did you die in this one?"

"The dream? I mean, it was going that way, but I woke up."

"Why do you think they're getting worse again?"

"I don't know." Graham covered his eyes with his hand. "I'm sorry. I know I sound crazy."

"Graham." Walt's voice was hard. "This is not something you can do alone. Now, how often do you see your therapist?"

"Once a month."

"That's not enough," he said shortly. "Can you see him every week?"

"My insurance won't cover it."

"Every other week, then. I'm serious, you can't mess around with this." He coughed again, violently, and Graham heard him gulping water after a moment. "You're not doing yourself any favors by letting this fester."

"I know," he sighed. He looked at the clock and thought about getting outside. Smoking a few cigarettes. He needed to think.

"Listen, tomorrow's Sunday," Walt continued in a softer tone. "Why don't I come over after Emerson goes home and we can have dinner or something?"

"Thanks, Walt. That'd be nice."

"Okay. But call me before then if you need anything."

"Sure," Graham responded, wishing he wasn't so fucking helpless. "I appreciate it."

17

It's starting to get cooler at night. You no longer wake up sweating, keeping a wet cloth handy to cool yourself down. Wondering how to steal a fan. You start to feel more like yourself.

In the morning, you map out your day. You've worked out a pretty good system. You still go to Yevgeny Alekseev's as often as possible, especially when Graham is working. It's been ten days since that final box, and you haven't spoken to him since, but he's started shielding you at the restaurant, letting you get in and out unnoticed. His presence has given you ideal security, so you accept the help and you're just glad he stopped coming by your place.

You saw a new Russian restaurant on your way home from Northside the other day, but it was late and it had already closed, so you go there first today.

It's called Taste of St. Petersburg and it has a gaudy neon sign. You go inside but it doesn't feel right. It's cramped and dirty and the chak-chak they have in the front case looks dry and stale. You sigh and know your aunt would never come here and you have to cross another place off your list. But you still ask. You always ask.

"Hi," you begin, making brief eye contact with the older woman behind the counter.

"What can I get you?"

There's no one else in the place and she's already impatient.

"I'm actually looking for someone."

"What?" she asks sharply, leaning over the counter. "Speak up."

"I'm looking for someone," you say a little louder, your face heating up. "A Russian woman named Lena. She's my aunt."

The woman behind the counter looks thoughtful, and when she speaks again her voice is softer.

"Lena what?"

"Mishnev. She's about forty, I guess."

"Patronymic?"

"Nicholskaya."

She rubs her chin, looking thoughtful again.

"Lena Nicholskaya," she murmurs. "Red hair, like you?"

You shake your head. "Black."

"Hold on," she says, and goes back to the kitchen where she starts questioning the cooks in rapid-fire Russian. You wait but it's making you nervous and you don't want to be there any longer. You know they can't help you.

"Sorry," she says when she returns a moment later. "Nobody's seen her."

You nod. "That's okay," you reply, forcing a smile and turning to leave. "Thanks for checking."

"You want some chak-chak to take?" she calls after you.

"No, thanks."

You hate it when they pity you, and it's almost made you stop looking for her. But if you stop, then you admit there are only two paths for you: going home or staying on the streets forever.

18

I ran away yesterday. I got a probability test back in math and I failed it. Really failed it. Mr. Thompson said I had to do corrections and get it signed by a parent. And I knew this would send him over the edge. He's been stressed about work and it always pisses him off when I have trouble in math because it comes so easy to him. But not everybody's meant to be a fucking engineer and I didn't want to deal with it so I didn't go home after school. I went to Britt's house and of course she said I could stay as long as I wanted and her parents wouldn't mind, so I said I'd stay the night and see how it goes. But around midnight I started to panic. I got the feeling I was just making everything worse for myself, and maybe I should just get it over with. So I went home. I had the test out and I was ready to tell him everything and get whatever was coming. I came in the back door and he was in the living room, watching Close Encounters. *He was drunk and high and started laughing when I walked over, saying he'd start the movie over and we could watch it together because it's fucking brilliant. I had this script worked out, though, and I couldn't really think clearly, so I still handed him the test and told him he'd need to sign it because I failed. He laughed again and told me to get him a pen. "You better not be getting dumber," he said as he wrote. "'Cause if you can't learn math, you'll be cleaning houses out of school. You get me?" I took back the test and saw he'd drawn a smiley face after his name. I watched the movie with him for a while until he passed out, and then I went to my room and cried till I fell asleep.*

You look at the date. That was only six months ago.

You put the journal down in your lap and pull your hair into a ponytail. You think about getting rid of it because reading your entries has never made you feel better about anything. But something makes you hang onto it, even write in it occasionally, and maybe if you wait long enough you'll have something good to write about.

You go back out in early afternoon, across Forty-Third to Yevgeny's. Graham's there, delivering drinks out on the back patio, when you arrive. You scan the area. No Lena. Graham looks better than usual and you think he might be getting more sleep, maybe going easier on the crack or angel dust or whatever it is he uses to take the edge off. You hang back a minute until he sees you. He gives a slight smile then turns away to clear a table. He stacks the empty plates on his tray and sets the ones with remaining food around the edge. You pretend to read the flyers advertising concerts and odd jobs and community events stuck around a lamp post while Graham sets the tray on an empty table in a vacant section. He jogs back inside, like he's forgotten something, and you know that's your cue to move in. There's so much leftover food on the plates—two intact rolls, a full side of fried mushrooms, and half a Rueben sandwich—you wonder if he chased away the patrons, knowing you'd be around soon. You wrap it all up and shove it in your bag before anyone sees, before he gets back.

You walk home confidently, feeling better about St. Petersburg and the journal because you always feel better when you get what you need without having to talk to anyone.

Matthias is crowded tonight, so you have to walk up and down a few times before you can slip into the alley unnoticed. It makes you nervous; you can't imagine what would bring this many people past your place. You think of Seventy-First. You know the patterns of your neighborhood pretty well, and as you reflect on the number of chances you've taken today—on most days—you can't help thinking it has something to do with you.

You hurry through the window, losing your balance on the milk crate in your haste. You stumble to the first light and turn it on. You walked the entire way home envisioning the nice meal you'd have, but now you've lost your appetite. You set the food aside and dig through the old cardboard box for your next book. You decide on *Catch-22* and bring it over to the wall opposite your window where your pillow is already propped up.

You read for an hour, hoping to relax and calm your mind enough to eat and sleep, but you feel it getting worse instead of better. You force yourself to take a few bites of the sandwich, but it tastes odd and metallic so you stop. You breathe slowly for a few minutes then go back to your book, but every time you try to focus the words become sinister to you. Your heartbeat quickens as you read what you're sure is a threat.

"You're no better than Mishnev."

"Who?"

"—yes, Raskolnikov, who—"

"Mishnev! Who . . . Doesn't matter; she ran. You know I could justify killing—"

You stop reading. You turn the page but the numbers aren't going in order anymore and maybe that's for you, too.

You sigh and rub you face with your hands. You can't do this. You're just a dumb kid trying to do this and what did you think would happen? That you'd find some way to live on your own? Get a job? Eat without stealing? How could you think you weren't just drawing out your own failure—making everything worse for yourself?

You don't know how those books made it to the corner of Forty-Ninth and Kingston, but you don't think anything's an accident anymore.

Chapter 19

Graham

Terminal Uniqueness

"Where are you today?"

Graham looked up and Dr. Schwartz was tapping his pen lightly against his notepad.

"I'm sorry?"

"It seems like your mind's someplace else. You didn't answer my question."

"What was your question?"

"Why didn't you take the bus? You said your bike is in the shop, and so you walked here. I said that's over fifty blocks and why didn't you just take the bus?"

Graham sighed, not wanting to go into it. He didn't want Schwartz to write any more notes or narrow his eyes or lean forward with concern.

"I can't," he finally answered.

"You can't?"

"It's just a little thing I have now," he dismissed with a shrug. "I can't use public transit; it's too crowded, and . . . I don't know . . ."

"How long has this been going on?" Schwartz was frowning now.

Graham laughed disdainfully. "Since New York."

Schwartz started writing again. "You've never brought it up before."

"Doesn't matter now," he replied. "I walk everywhere. If it's really far I ride my bike."

"What about Emerson? Don't you take her places? What about when you need to drop her off at Anna's?"

"It's really not a big deal." Graham was starting to get annoyed. "Lots of times Anna picks her up, or we'll take a cab. And we walk most places around here."

"Cabs are okay?"

"Yeah." Graham looked up at the clock, as he often did, focusing on the gentle tick of the second hand and hoping Schwartz would move on.

"All right." Schwartz wrote a few more things down. "So, tell me about New York."

"What do you mean?"

"You said this has been happening since you lived in New York. Can you remember the first time?"

Graham watched the pen resting in his therapist's hand and desperately wanted to forget it. But he needed a change. Things were getting worse, just as Schwartz had said they would, and Graham didn't want to start over again.

"I was late to start the semester, you know, at culinary school," he began reluctantly. "I didn't think I'd be doing college at all, but my parents thought it would snap me out of it. We didn't have a lot of money, but—"

"Graham, you're dodging again," Schwartz interrupted. "I know all this already."

"I'm leading up to it, all right?"

"That's fine, but we're still working on you giving direct answers, so I'm going to mention it when I see it."

"Fine," Graham muttered. He leaned back. Schwartz had thrown him off and he'd lost his momentum.

"Tell me about the first time," he repeated.

"I'd gone out with one of my friends from school. Sal. We'd walk to the bars around Soho all the time. This first time, though, I'd only been in New York a few weeks, and I was nervous about school and living away from home." He stopped. He didn't know how to proceed and didn't want Schwartz to think even less of him.

"Did you drink too much?"

Graham nodded. "Yeah."

"Was Sal worried about you?"

"No. He never mentioned it."

"So, what happened?"

"When it was time to go home I could barely walk. Sal said we could just take the Broadway Main Line to Canal Street—it would take five minutes. But I started crying, and I begged him not to make me get on the subway. Just thinking about it made me start to relive the accident. He helped me get to an alley so I could throw up, then he helped me walk home. He had to support most of my weight over his shoulders."

"And he never mentioned it after that?"

Graham shook his head.

"But it happened again."

"Several times."

"Did he ever tell you you'd had too much to drink?"

"No. He wasn't like that."

"What about your roommate?"

"Ira didn't really come out with us. But I know he heard me sometimes, at night. I'd wake up from a nightmare and I know he must have heard me shouting. Those walls were pretty thin."

"But he never mentioned anything either."

"That's right."

"Do you think that's odd? These were your closest friends."

Graham shrugged. "They just weren't like that."

"Okay," Schwartz replied, but he started writing again and Graham knew there was more he wanted to say. "Did you keep in contact with them after you left school?"

"No."

"Do you think losing them contributed to your breakdown?"

"It wasn't really a breakdown."

"You overdosed on sleeping pills."

"I was really tired."

Schwartz smiled. "We could do an hour on your defensive humor alone."

Graham looked down, wanting to lead him away from this but not sure how.

"And that's when you first had trouble with fire, right?" he continued. "That's when you disconnected your gas range and quit smoking to get away from it."

"I guess. Listen," he said, scratching his head, "don't you want to hear about something else?"

"Like what?"

"I don't know. Emerson's been doing better lately."

"That's great."

"She's going to be in a play at school. She hasn't done that in a few years."

"What's the play?"

"*Rikki-Tikki Tavi.*"

"Great. Good for her." Schwartz set his notepad on the desk behind him. "How's the girl from the restaurant?"

Graham's smile faded. "She's not talking to me."

"Why?"

"I came on too strong," he said, looking away. It made him sick to remember and was sure Schwartz could tell. "I made her think I was some kind of predator," he continued, rubbing his forehead, "and now she just wants me to leave her alone. So that's what I'm doing."

"Were you inappropriate with her?"

"No. Jesus, Mel," Graham winced. "I just asked her to come by the restaurant at closing so she could pick up the extra food. I didn't think about how late it would be. She thought I was trying to get her alone." He sighed. "You really think I would do that?"

"No," Schwartz said simply. "But I'm constantly surprised in this job. And I know there's a lot you keep from me."

Graham looked back up at the clock to avoid his gaze. It was hard to deny.

20

You walk south on Matthias but decide to turn west on Thirty-Ninth Street for a change. You can't get too comfortable. You look around at the ramshackle shops and businesses. You're not watching where you're going and nearly run into a woman passing by. You raise your eyes and glance at the people ahead of you.

Then you see him.

You feel a jolt of pain in your chest.

It's him.

It's over.

Walking ahead of you, he's walking right ahead of you. You recognize his thick shock of a ponytail, his worn gray jacket. He turns to the side for a moment and you see his profile. His dark beard. His quick, discerning eyes. *Will he kill me here or bring me back first?* You slow your pace and allow a few more people to walk in front of you. There's static in your ears. When you're able to force your body into action you turn and run the other way, unsure of where you're going.

Graham sees you coming a couple of blocks away. He doesn't usually seem interested, but you're running. You haven't slowed down even though your breath is short and your legs feel numb. You know you look crazy. You might be crying. Dark spots dance in front of your eyes. Graham takes the arm of one of the waitresses and points to his table, whispering something to her. Then, as you finally near the restaurant, he gestures for you to meet him at the back of the building.

You collapse onto a folding chair to catch your breath. Graham lights a cigarette. He hands you a bottle of water and you take a drink. You lean over and cover your face with your hands and try to focus on breathing normally. You feel a hand on your back and jump up, knocking over the chair.

"Whoa," Graham says gently. "What's going on? Why were you running like that?"

"He's here."

You're shaking all over, from the running and the shock, so you set up the chair and Graham helps you sit without falling.

"Who's here?"

"My dad. I need to get out of the city."

Graham looks past you out onto the street, as if he would immediately see and recognize this person. He doesn't say anything, though, he just gets this stern look and you know he's mad at you. You said you didn't need him and now here you are.

"I have to do it now," you say. "I've got to leave and I need help. I mean, just a bus ticket. I can pay you back whenever I get where I'm going. It doesn't matter where."

"Your dad," he repeats evenly.

"Yeah."

You look down. It's not going like you thought and now you're regretting the whole thing. But he's your only option.

"I just thought, I don't know, I thought maybe it was a group home you'd left. That kind of thing."

You don't have time for this. "Can I have the money?"

He swallows hard and shakes his head. There's a sinking feeling in your stomach.

"Are you mad at me or something?" you demand, trying not to cry. "Why are you being a dick?"

Graham looks down, as if he hadn't even heard you. He brings his cigarette to his mouth and you see his hand is shaking.

"What did he do?"

"It doesn't matter now." You look at him directly, trying to get through. "He's going to kill me, Graham."

His eyes finally meet yours and his voice is hard.

"I'm not going to let that happen."

You pause. "You're not mad at me?"

"No," he murmurs, rubbing his eyes. "No, I'm not mad at you." He sits on a chair across from you. "What's his name?"

"My dad? Casey."

"Last name?"

"What do you want with him?"

"I don't know. I really just . . . I don't know. I'd like to straighten him out, though."

"I wouldn't want you to go to jail."

Graham smiles and seems to relax a little. "I think that's the nicest thing you've said to me."

"So you'll help me?"

He nods. "Of course."

"I can have the money?"

"I don't think you should leave town."

"What? What do you mean?" You feel your ears heat up and you try not to yell. "I just fucking saw him on Thirty-Ninth, and you think I should stick around? Are you new here?"

Graham smiles but his eyes are still serious.

"It's too dangerous, doing all this by yourself. If you try to set all this up again in a new place, you're liable to be found out. I mean, it'd be different if you were almost eighteen and could just hold out until then." He studies you carefully. "Really, how old are you?

You narrow your eyes.

"Fourteen."

"I think you should stay with me. For a while, at least."

"Are you serious?"

"Yeah."

"I'm not looking for another dad."

"I don't blame you," he replies. He hands you back the water you dropped and you notice he's wearing a bracelet. Pink and yellow rubber bands braided together. "How about a much older brother?"

You glance back at the street, but no one's there. You look at Graham. *This is wrong.* This is what you're running from.

"No," you say, shaking your head. "I can't."

He frowns. "But you need help."

"I've been looking for my aunt," you say, remembering why you came here in the first place.

He pauses, and looks confused at the change of subject.

"Your aunt?"

"Yeah."

"What's her name?"

"Lena Mishnev."

"You think she's been by the restaurant?"

"I don't know. I don't know if she even lives here."

"We could try to find her," he offers, but his voice sounds hollow.

You shake your head again as you stand, suddenly feeling trapped. You can't just believe what he says. You can't just trust him.

"No, it's fine," you say slowly. "I just need to be more careful. I-I'm sorry I asked you for the money."

"Hey, it's all right," he murmurs, coming toward you with that unbearable look of pity in his eyes. "We can figure something out."

All at once, the air around you is suffocating. You can see the particles, floating and dividing, and the stale heat sits on your chest. You blink, but they're still there. You know this is wrong—that you shouldn't be seeing air like this, and it means you're losing whatever game it is you've been forced into playing. You take another drink and close your eyes. You count to ten.

"I have to go," you mutter. You open your eyes. The particles are gone. "I have to go."

"But what about Casey?"

"I'll be more careful."

He doesn't believe you and now he's watching you and thinking you're an idiot for getting into all this in the first place. But he's not safe and now you have to get out of there. You start edging away.

"This is too dangerous," he says. "Let me help you."

You turn and run. You don't stop until you get to your warehouse on Matthias. You start shoving things into your backpack. You think about how you'll steal the money for a bus ticket. You need to be more careful.

21

That night is the hardest you can remember. You keep hearing a rustling outside your window, and keep checking on it, but no one is ever there. There's a soft hum in your ears and the light is too bright from the bulbs on the ceiling, so you turn them all off and try to ignore the shadows thrown on the wall by the streetlight. You sit up all night, leaning against the concrete wall under the window. You think you might have drifted off for a few minutes because you hear your dad's voice, telling you it's time to come home, that nothing bad will happen if you give up now. It gives you a jolt, hearing that voice, and then you start to think you couldn't have fallen asleep because only two minutes have passed on your watch and your rushing adrenaline won't let you relax. *He's here.* The wind picks up outside and you jump at the sound of the old wooden boards banging against the building.

It's over, kiddo. Just admit it.

Electricity shoots through your temples and you cry out. You jump off the milk crate and look around frantically. It's like he's in your head. You stand on the crate and look out the window. You're relieved to see the sky is turning a hazy gray and your watch says it's 5:15. The world will wake up soon and people will start walking up and down Matthias and you won't have to be alone anymore. You think about getting a little sleep so you lie down on your blanket and close your eyes, but the humming that's still in your head grows shriller and starts to grate on your ears. And you worry that you're exposed.

You eat some dry cereal and drink a little water. You hear rustling again. *Graham should have given me the money,* you think wistfully. *I could be on a bus by now.* You think about the next city you'd try—some place your aunt would have chosen—but you know there are so many possibilities that it doesn't even matter what you decide. The rustling gets louder and your head is pounding and you hear your dad say your name over and over in your mind, like a demonic chant intended to drive you insane, so you move to the opposite wall and slide down to the floor, covering your ears.

"Hey, are you in there?"

The words are muffled, so you uncover your ears and silently move behind the water heater, unsure of who said them. Your heart is slamming. You don't have a plan for this.

"Hello? Can I come in?

You breathe deeply and move out of the shadows. *Graham.* You step up on the crate and uncover the window. You've never been so relieved to see someone, but you force yourself to remember he's still a stranger.

"Yeah," you reply slowly, your voice hoarse. "Yeah, come in."

He carefully slides through the window and lowers himself to the floor. He looks around. You don't think he's slept either.

"I'm sorry," he begins—the way he always begins, "I know I said I wouldn't come here again, and I really won't after this, I just had to see if you were all right."

You look at the floor and don't say anything because you can feel the knot rising from your stomach to your throat and you don't trust yourself to speak.

"Are you all right?" he asks after a moment. "I mean, did you have any trouble last night?"

You want to laugh. You can't remember the last night you didn't have any trouble. But you look at his face and it's clear he's tired and worried and you know what he means and you wish you could explain what's going on in your head but you'd cry or throw up before you got through it.

"I didn't sleep," you say finally. "I kept hearing things." You pause. "I heard his voice."

"Do you think he was here?" Graham asks, suddenly alert.

You nod. "I know he's still close."

You think about it and about what it means for you and suddenly the emotion of everything hits you. You turn away from Graham and let your face distort as the tears well up. You wish he would leave now, but if he tried you'd probably beg him to stay. It's finally becoming clear how weak you are.

"Hey," he says gently. You hear him walking toward you. "It's okay."

You laugh. You shake your head and turn around.

"I am absolutely fucked." You wipe your eyes and nose with your sleeves. "I should never have tried this."

"When did you leave?"

"A couple months ago. Almost three, I guess."

"I think you've done okay."

"Doesn't matter now."

He turns back toward the window and you get a fleeting stab of fear that he's going to leave, but he sits down on the milk crate and runs his hands through his hair. He's wearing jeans, so you know he doesn't have to be at work soon. The laces of his tennis shoes have broken and been retied in knots, and his Raiders t-shirt is so thin it's likely older than you are. You think he's probably lived here his whole life.

"Will you reconsider? Think about staying with me for a while?"

His voice is low and calm and you can't picture him ever raising it. He's looking at you and something about him seems so sad you wonder why he's really doing this.

You shake your head. "I don't know you," you say helplessly.

"I know," he replies. "I don't know you, either. But something is going on here, and I can't just ignore it. I mean, what if it was my daughter in trouble? I'd hope someone would reach out to her."

"If it was your daughter, you'd want somebody to bring her back to you," you respond warily.

"That's fair. But I promise you, I'm not sympathizing with your dad." Graham frowns. "I can see that's not where you should be. I just don't want you to get hurt out here."

"Does your daughter live with you?"

"Some weekends and holidays. She visits a few evenings a week, too."

You pause. "You think I'll be found out if I stay here?"

"I'm not sure. I just think you can't do this alone anymore."

You sigh. He's right. And you will be found out. He's been closing in on you for a long time and now there's nowhere to hide. You scan the warehouse once more before turning back to Graham.

"Okay, yes."

"Really?" He looks at you directly now, with clear surprise. "You'll give it a try?"

You nod, the weight lifting from your throat but leaving reverberations of dizziness and trembling.

"Yes. Thank you," you murmur.

"Great," he says, radiating relief. He stands up. "I've got to get to the restaurant. Do you think you can stay here until my shift is over? Just three hours, then I can pick you up."

"The restaurant?" you frown. "But you're not dressed for it."

"I know," he laughs, looking down. "I'm washing dishes today. One of the guys really needed a sub, and no one else could do it."

"I should stay here?" you repeat hollowly, suddenly feeling your exhaustion. You nod slowly. "Okay."

But you have no confidence left. And the last thing you want to do is stay in the warehouse alone. You don't meet his eyes.

"Would you rather come with me?" he asks, as if reading your thoughts. "It's no problem. You could hang out on that back patio where I take my breaks."

You shake your head, ready to tell him that's silly; you've lived this way for nearly three months and you can certainly stay in your own home in broad daylight by yourself. But you can't. The words never come and you're left with a pained expression and that familiar stinging in your eyes.

"It's okay," Graham says quickly. "You should come."

"Will Jack be there?"

Graham smiles. "Not today. I'll just let everyone know my niece is out of school early and nobody will bother you." He glances around. "We'll pick up your stuff after, okay?"

You nod gratefully, but you're not sure how to feel about the decision you've made. You're not sure how to feel about anything anymore.

22

Graham's place is nicer than you thought it would be: a third floor walk-up on Prospect Avenue with a view of the courtyard. He shows you the bathroom and gives you a new toothbrush and says you can use the shower and the towels and the peach lotion on the counter, if you want. He tells you to set your things in the second bedroom. It's yellow with butterfly decals on the wall.

"Where's your daughter going to stay?"

"In with me."

"She won't mind?"

"She's only eight. She still likes me."

You walk by Graham's room. He has an old wooden dresser with a small television set on top. A bed with a navy comforter wadded up in the middle. You follow him into the kitchen. He opens the fridge and pulls out two oranges, handing you one.

"No beer?" you ask, peering inside.

He smiles. "I wasn't expecting guests."

"So, what, you're into harder stuff?" you ask, glancing at the upper cabinets. "Gin, vodka, that kind of thing?"

He shakes his head. "No." He walks over and opens up the cabinets for you to see. Cereal. Coffee. Cups with crazy straws. "I don't drink, actually."

"Not at all?"

He sits down at the kitchen table and offers you a chair.

"No. It's not my thing."

You sit next to him and start peeling your orange. Graham's peeling his, too, with an amused kind of look on his face, as you take in more of the apartment. There's rooster border paper along the ceiling and a plaid dishtowel hanging from a hook. A Wile E. Coyote cookie jar on the counter catches your eye.

"What do you keep in there?" You nod toward the jar.

"Candy," he replies. "Mostly Chick-O-Sticks. Those are my daughter's favorite."

"What's her name?"

"Emerson."

There's silence for a minute and you're wondering how much of what he says is true. If he really doesn't drink. If he's really so devoted to his daughter.

"You can meet her this weekend," Graham says, briefly rising from the table to toss his peel. "She'll be here after school on Friday."

"Okay." You pick at a splinter of wood on the table.

"You like kids?"

You shrug. "I guess."

"Do you have any brothers or sisters?"

"Nope."

You start to feel a little claustrophobic so you stand up and ask Graham if you can go lie down. He doesn't mind.

In your room—Emerson's room—it's so quiet you can hear the clock tick. The bed is soft and it feels good to lie down but your heart pounds. You're gripped by a terrible feeling and your first instinct is to run. Get out. Go back to the warehouse. You have to force yourself to breathe, to remember you don't have another option.

You pull a blanket and pillow off the bed and lie down on the floor. That's a little better, but the buzzing is back in your ears. You unzip your backpack and pull out your journal. You scan quickly to where you left off.

The light bulb.

You tap your pen against the paper.

I hadn't heard him at first. He'd said the bulb over the kitchen table had burned out, but it was hard to hear over the television. Dateline. I thought he was saying something about the show so I nodded in agreement, but that was a mistake. "Well, then, get the fuck up and fix it!" he yelled. Luckily he also pointed, so I knew what he meant. I set my books aside; I wasn't going to be able to study anyway. The TV always got louder as it got later and he got drunker. Fuck him, I thought. I'll change his light bulb, but that's it. Maybe then I can get something done in my room. I got a new bulb from the closet and stood on a chair to screw it in. I know now that I should have just gotten up on the table, because the chair was rickety and the height was making my hands shake, but it started to screw in so I kept at it.

Then I dropped the light bulb. The sweat from my hand greased it, made me think it was tightening, but it fell onto the table and shattered. I stared at it for just a second before I jumped down and ran for the door, but it was too long. I'll never know how a man weighed down by a fifth of gin could move so fast. He slammed me into the wall then slipped and fell hard. He held his arm and started cursing. I was going to pay for that, too.

I can't remember if I started out apologizing, or crying, or trying to match his rage with attitude. It doesn't ever matter. This time was worse because he'd hurt himself. Much worse. I was sneezing blood for three days. I wasn't allowed to leave the apartment that whole week, the last week of school. I thought about buying poison, or a gun. I didn't know if it would be for him or for me. So I left.

There's a knock at the door and you automatically shove your journal under the bed.

"Come in."

"Hey," Graham murmurs, opening the door hesitantly. "Were you sleeping?"

You shake your head and try to appear normal. You don't know how long you were in there.

"Are you okay?"

You blink rapidly and nod, wishing he would stop looking at you.

"Was there something wrong with the bed?"

"I just like the floor."

"Well, are you ready for dinner?"

You tilt your head slightly, confused. "Dinner?"

"Yeah, it's nearly seven. Are you hungry?"

The buzzing in your ears is loud and it's hard for you to concentrate.

"Is it crowded?"

"What?" Graham comes in. He's standing above you now and his face is dark.

"Yevgeny's," you stammer. He's between you and the door. "I shouldn't go in if it's crowded. I don't usually come at dinnertime." You stare past him, trying to think. "I should go home."

"Wait," he begins slowly. "Yevgeny's? I mean, we were there earlier, but . . ." he trails off, frowning. "You had to leave the warehouse. We're in my apartment now. Remember? This is Emerson's room."

You look around. The yellow. The butterflies. You take a few breaths and close your eyes, and when you open them Graham looks a little softer to you.

He sits on the edge of the bed. You remember the kitchen now—the roosters, Wile E. Coyote, the crazy straws. You don't know where your mind was. You rub your eyes and feel a little better. Your hearing is getting back to normal and you can smell something on the stove.

"I know," you reply. "I guess maybe I did fall asleep for a few minutes. I just . . . I forgot."

"It's okay. There's been a lot going on." He smiles and you hope he'll forget the whole thing.

Graham stands up and tries again—asks you if you're ready for dinner. You rise to your feet as well and gingerly rub your side. You nod and follow him to the kitchen. He made chili. From a recipe. He opens the oven and pulls out cornbread. Hunger is now a constant state to you, something you don't even think about anymore. You fill your plate and bring it to the table but Graham gets a funny little smile and asks you if you want to watch a movie while you eat.

"It's something we'd do sometimes when I was a kid," he said. "I always thought that was the coolest thing, being able to eat in the living room."

"Sure."

You set up your food on the end table by the recliner and Graham opens up a cabinet under the TV to show you the movies. You get to pick. You sit on the floor and scan the titles. You wonder if he'd let you pick an R-rated one, but you really don't want to watch those. You pull out *Ghostbusters*. It was Britt's favorite. You watched it at her house two weeks before you left.

"Great," he says, turning on the VCR. "Seen it before?"

"I think so."

You sit in the recliner and he takes the couch. Your mind is settled and you start to eat. It's the first complete meal you've had in months. And you can eat until you're full. You sit back in the chair and after a while sense that something has changed. You look over at Graham. He's laughing and reminds you of a little kid. He really could be your older brother. You smile.

Toward the end of the movie he goes into the kitchen and comes back with a handful of Chick-O-Sticks. He hands you a few. He says he'll refill it for Emerson.

You spend the next half hour drifting in and out of sleep. He shakes your shoulder and you jolt awake.

"Hey, I'm going to bed," he says softly.

You look around. The TV's off, he's already taken your dishes.

"Okay." You get up slowly. "Thanks, for dinner."

"You're welcome." He turns to leave. "Good night."

You watch Graham go, but when he reaches the bedroom door you stop him.

"Wait," you say, still unsure of yourself. He turns back around. "My name's Laika."

You can tell he's as tired as you are, but he smiles broadly. And, in a rare occurrence, you don't regret what you've done.

23

Graham wakes you up the next morning to tell you he's going to work. He says he knocked on the door but you didn't answer, so he came in and found you sleeping on the floor. You sit up and look at the clock. 11:35.

"What should I do?" you ask groggily.

He shrugs. "Whatever you want. There's cereal and that kind of thing in the kitchen. And—"

"Hold on," you stop him, narrowing your eyes. "You're letting me stay here by myself?"

"That's right."

"You're not worried I'll steal something?"

Graham laughs. "Not really."

You rummage through your backpack, looking for a hair tie. You haven't unpacked anything. You keep your clothes in the same cardboard box they were in back at the warehouse, and your only other possessions fit in your bag. It just doesn't seem right, taking over his daughter's room.

"So, you'll be all right?" he asks, stuffing his wallet in his back pocket and adjusting his tie.

You nod.

"It's a long shift today," he continues, glancing at the clock. "I won't be back till about eleven tonight."

"Okay."

"Do you have a keychain?"

You frown. "Yeah, I think so."

You unzip the front pouch of your backpack and pull it out to show him. It's a badly scratched plastic dog you've had since fourth grade. It still has your old apartment key on it. You forgot about that.

"Here." He kneels down and starts winding a key around the ring. "If you decide to leave, lock the door behind you, okay? And keep it safe so you don't get locked out."

It's clear he's used to talking to an eight-year-old.

"Okay," you say slowly.

You look down. The key looks just like your old one. You immediately take yours off the ring. If you need to get into the apartment in a hurry, you don't want to mix them up. Graham is looking at you. That buzzing is building up again and you're starting to feel overwhelmed. The key is hot in your hand. *What is he doing? It's part of a plan; it has to be.*

"Do you need anything, before I go?"

You shake your head. You could barely make out what he was saying. You just want him to leave. You need to think.

Chapter 24

Graham

Either You Are or You Aren't

"So, has it been one night, or two?" Anna probed, narrowing her eyes at Graham.

"What are you talking about?"

"I can tell you haven't slept. I just can't figure out how many nights it's been."

Graham looked away and his mouth twitched into a brief smile. He watched her hang her purse on the back of the chair. Her twill office dress looked good and her eyes were bright, so he was sure she'd had no trouble sleeping lately.

"Two," he said finally. "I've had worse."

"Still . . ." She tilted her head sympathetically. "I'm sorry. Do you want to order something?" she asked, gesturing to the counter behind him. "I mean, this is your dinner break, right?"

"I'll eat back at work. Coffee's fine for me."

"All right," she replied, watching him thoughtfully again. "So, what's going on? Why'd you want to meet again so soon?"

Graham took a breath. He wasn't sure how to begin. Dread and insecurity weighed him down, which was nothing new. He would often come in to his meetings with Anna with a gray fog clouding his mind because he'd spent days working himself up over an issue with Emerson: an oddity in her speech, a concerning reaction, any change in mood he'd noticed during their time together, but he always left feeling better. Anna had a way of putting things in perspective; she would calm him down and give him a few hopeful counterexamples, and his fears would be assuaged. But now Graham worried this would be too much, even for her.

"Did something happen with Emerson?"

He understood that note of worry had crept into her voice because he was just sitting there, his tired, red eyes barely registering the world around him. And she still thought this was about Emerson.

"No," he assured her. "She's fine. She's actually seemed better lately."

"I've thought that, too." Anna took a drink of tea, relaxing slightly. "So, what is it, then?"

"Well," he began, shifting in his chair as he searched for the right words. "There's this other girl I've been worried about. Her name's Laika. She used to come by the restaurant a lot, taking scraps of food. She was actually pretty good at it." He smiled, absently swirling his coffee around in the cup. "I haven't really talked to her until recently, but I think she's in a lot of trouble."

"So, she's homeless?" Anna frowned. "How old is she?"

"Fourteen."

"What did she tell you?"

"Not much, the first couple times. After she'd been coming a few weeks, though, I knew there was something wrong, so I followed her. She's been sleeping in some warehouse—a real shitty place on the west side. I just kept thinking about Emerson, you know?" He rubbed his forehead. "I think she might have some kind of spectrum thing, too, just from what I've seen of her, and it killed me to think of Emerson trying to live like that."

He looked up at Anna, trying to gauge her reaction so far, but she could be a tough read. She looked concerned, like she really cared about what happened to this kid, but maybe that was just confusion. He knew she was wondering why he was telling her all this—what it had to do with them.

"Anyway," Graham continued, "I left her a few boxes of stuff while she was gone. Just some basic food and a few hand-me-downs from Dawn. And some books."

"You left her stuff?" Anna broke in, still frowning. "Did you say it was from you?"

"No."

"Graham," she chided, drawing out his name into two annoyed syllables. "You probably scared the shit out of her."

"I know. I didn't think about that. And I felt bad, because she did think I was some kind of weirdo, but I knew she needed help. I just—I had to help her. I didn't know what else to do."

Anna nodded and his confidence increased a bit.

"So, a couple of days ago," he continued, his voice lowering, "she came by the restaurant. But it was different. She didn't want food; she told me she had to get out of town. She said her dad was after her and she'd just seen him out on the street. She wanted money for a bus ticket."

"Jesus," Anna breathed. "Did you give it to her?"

Graham shook his head, avoiding her eyes. "I told her she should stay with me."

Anna laughed. "Are you serious?"

"Yeah."

"There's no way she went for that."

"No," he admitted. "She ran away. But the next day—yesterday—I went to see her, just to check on how she was doing. She'd been up all night, standing guard, I guess. She was making herself sick, thinking this guy was going to find her."

"So you asked her again."

Graham nodded, looking at Anna carefully now. "I hope this is okay with you. She said she'd give it a try. I'm letting her stay in Emerson's room, and Emerson can just stay in with me on her weekends. I think it's important," he added.

Anna was silent, thinking, but only for a moment. "This isn't safe," she said, shaking her head. "What about Emerson? What if this girl is dangerous?"

"She's not."

"Graham, you don't know her. I mean, what has she been through? What was going on with the father?"

"She wouldn't tell me. But in the apartment she got nervous looking around the kitchen. She kept asking me what I drank, what I was into, trying to find the liquor and beer. I think he's an alcoholic. And I'm sure he's violent."

Anna rested her chin in her hand. Her gaze went past Graham and he knew she was weighing the different parts of this, just as he had.

"They'd never be alone together," he offered gently. "At night, Emerson will sleep on the fold-out in my room and I'll be right there. But I really don't think there's any reason to worry. She's just a scared kid. She needs a safe place, for a little while at least."

"We should go to the police," Anna said. "She should at least be in school. And if she does have something like a spectrum disorder, she'll need to see somebody."

"The police will fuck this up," he said firmly. "You know that. If Casey covers his tracks, they'll give her to him—"

"Who's Casey?"

"Her dad."

"Did she tell you their last name?"

"No. I asked, but she didn't want me to attack him and go to jail."

"Lovely," she scoffed. "I'm really getting on board with this whole thing."

"She said she *didn't* want me to attack him. I think that's big of her."

"I think you've got a blind spot for this girl that's not letting you see what could go wrong."

"What I'm saying," Graham continued, ignoring her, "is if the police send her back with her dad, she's fucked. And if they give her up to the state, who knows what will happen? She needs an advocate."

"Is that even legal?" she asked, setting aside her empty mug. "Having her stay with you?"

"I don't know. But I think it's right. And she mentioned an aunt she's been looking for. I can try to help her with that, and maybe she'll end up in a stable home."

"Well, what if we help out? I mean, maybe she could stay at Barry's place. It's not that far from you."

"That's nice," he smiled, imagining Barry's reaction to such a proposal, "but I don't think so. Laika is incredibly slow to trust, and Barry's not exactly a warm and fuzzy kind of guy."

"He's great with Emerson," Anna retorted defensively. "Is this because he wouldn't give you his home number? You really can't blame him for wanting to avoid your midnight calls, Graham."

"No, no," he smiled, "it's not that. It's just that it's taken a long time to get to this point, to have her trust me like this. I feel responsible now."

"You don't have to."

"And, actually, it's not just that," Graham murmured, adjusting his coffee cup on the table. "My nightmares have been getting worse. I mean, back to how they were three or four years ago, remember?"

Anna nodded, her eyes softening with concern.

"And I've been having trouble lighting matches again," he smiled scornfully. "All that shit. So, the other night I was up and called Walt, and he asked me why I thought it was getting worse and I told him I didn't know. But I think it's everything that's been going on with Laika. These visions keep pounding me at night, reminding me of how useless I was. How I let people die." He looked away, shaking his head. "Maybe it's getting worse because I know I have the chance to help somebody now. Maybe I'm supposed to start making up for everything. I know it's selfish, but I need to make up for it, you know?"

Anna leaned over and took his hand. "I know."

Graham looked up gratefully, relieved she seemed to be coming around. Relieved he might have one less thing to worry about.

"So, it's okay with you? She can stay for a while?"

Anna nodded slightly. "I want to meet her, though. Soon. Whenever you think it wouldn't freak her out."

"Absolutely."

"I hope it helps," she said, as if resigning herself to the decision.

"I know it will," he replied, taking a sip of his refilled coffee.

"You're a good person," she remarked. "Not a lot of people would do this."

"Well, like I said, it's not just for her."

Anna smiled and, as usual, Graham couldn't tell what she was thinking. He checked the clock above the espresso machine.

"Do you have to get back?" she asked.

"Not yet," he said, leaning back in his chair. "Tell me about you and Barry."

"What?" she laughed. "That sounds awful. Why would you want to hear about us?"

"I'm just curious," he replied with an innocent smile. "It's been, what, two years? Three?"

"About two."

"That's pretty serious."

"Yes," she nodded slowly. "We're serious."

"You think you'll marry him?"

"Probably."

"You don't sound thrilled."

"Maybe because it's weird as shit talking about this with you." She threw her napkin at him and he laughed.

"Sorry, I just want to know if this guy could be my kid's new dad some-day."

"No," she said seriously. "No, she'll never have a new dad, no matter who the guy is."

Graham nodded, rubbing the back of his neck. "Thanks."

"I should go," Anna said, looking at the clock and rising from her chair. "My shift starts soon."

"Me, too." He smiled as she walked toward the entrance. "Say 'hi' to Billy for me," he called.

She held up her middle finger and walked out the door without looking back, and Graham couldn't deny how much he missed her.

25

It's strange not having to scrounge for food. You're not quite sure what your purpose is now. As soon as Graham leaves you start walking around the apartment. You notice three packs of cigarettes high on a bookshelf, a political thriller on his nightstand, a woman's phone number taped to the fridge. Not much to go on. *Anna.* Another number in the top corner. "90–90." You frown at it. You go through all the cabinets and drawers in the kitchen. Lots of coffee, lots of rice. You dig to the back of the cabinets but you can't find the alcohol. You'll check the closets.

He keeps a surprising amount of fresh produce. You expected to find mostly microwave dinners and boxed meals from a guy who lives alone. You think for a minute. You remember the dinner he made. *Maybe he wants to move up at the restaurant.* You throw out the expired mayonnaise and move on to his bedroom.

The drawers of his dresser are warped so you have to shove them back and forth to get them open. Clothes, wadded up and crammed in. *No wonder he always looks like hell.* There are a few more books in the nightstand, a crime novel and a biography on FDR. There's also a parent handbook for Westmoreland Elementary School and a pair of drugstore reading glasses. You open the door to his closet. Just the clothes he wears to work along with a few pairs of jeans and heavier shirts. Ties crowded onto one hanger, a few crumpled on the floor. Three belts on a wobbly shelf. You move a stack of folded sheets and blankets from the floor out of your way, revealing a file cabinet. You pull at the drawer. Locked. Your heart beats a little faster. You knew he was hiding something.

You look around the room, wondering where to start looking for the key. You go back through his dresser drawers more carefully. You inspect the closet walls and shelves. You open the drawer to his nightstand again, taking out his books. You stop. You'd thought the drawer was only as deep as the books, but now you see a crumpled, empty cigarette pack was hidden behind them. You take it out and shake it. It's not empty. You turn it over and the small, silver key falls into your hand. You're sweating now as the blood fiercely pounds in your head.

But you already know what you'll find. You walk back to the closet, realizing you were right to be suspicious of him. You know what you're doing. You know he seems like a good guy, but his schedule-one narcotics and hard liquor are about to betray him. You shove the key into the cabinet's lock and you're no longer nervous. You're angry.

You frown as the drawer opens to reveal a number of shoeboxes. They're labeled. You kneel down and pull the first one out. EMERSON.

You're confused as you look through several drawings, mostly of birds and dogs and scenes from Disney movies. A few are done in crayon or pencil, but they're mostly marker on faded construction paper. A few birthday cards with little kid writing scrawled across the inside. There's a photograph of Graham holding her at a birthday party. You think she's maybe four or five, but you're bad at guessing kids' ages. He's wearing sunglasses and smiling and looking at something off to the side, out of the picture. There are a few school pictures, and one of her at a petting zoo. There's a program from a school play. *Charlie and the Chocolate Factory*. She was an Oompa Loompa.

You set it aside. You have no idea why he felt the need to lock up that kind of thing. You turn back to the file cabinet. The other boxes don't look very interesting, but that probably means their hiding something. RECEIPTS. A few appliance repairs, donations to Goodwill, grocery store receipts, clothes, a bike, bike repair. INSURANCE is next. Renter's insurance paperwork. Co-pays to the doctor, flu shots, physicals, child check-ups, strep tests, counseling.

Counseling.

You frown. The paper doesn't say why. It doesn't say if it was Graham. *Maybe for Emerson, after the divorce.* You put the box away.

NYC. You're not sure what to expect from this one, but looking through it you gather he lived there before Emerson. He looks young from the few pictures you find, maybe in college, out in the city with friends. Most of the pictures are taken at night, slightly blurry, in front of neon-lit bars and theater marquees. You flip through and find a few of him in another apartment—cooking an intricate-looking meal in one, sitting on the couch with a pretty girl in another. There are ticket stubs for Broadway shows, concerts, movies, fliers for bands playing at nightclubs. You replace the lid slowly and pull out the last box: BILLS, PAID.

An innocuous title that sounds boring as shit. But you open the box to find it's filled with letters. Folded in thirds, lined up neatly. No drugs. You look around nervously. It's not that you feel bad about going through his stuff—you're used to cutting ethical corners in order to stay safe—but your heart is racing again because you know you've found something important. Something that can help make sense out of this. You don't know if they're in any order but you'd better keep them the way they are. You take one from the left side and open it carefully.

5/21/91

Dear Emerson,

I don't know where to begin. I had such an amazing weekend with you, and I'm constantly in awe of what a funny and loving person you are. I'm sorry the science center was closed, but you were a trooper about it, and the zoo was a great replacement. I don't know how much longer you'll let me (or I'll be able to) carry you on my shoulders, so I'm enjoying it while I can. On the way out we passed a little boy in a wheelchair and you asked me if his dad would hold him up like that to see the animals. I said I thought he would, but you wanted to stay in case he needed me to do it for him. You have such a kind soul and I hope you're always so willing to share it.

I've been meaning to write more often, I'm sorry it will be several months between letters. I've been feeling much better, though. I really do enjoy working at the restaurant (someday we'll eat there together, but I don't think you'll like the food yet), and I'm hoping to move up to line cook soon. It's hard, knowing I can do so much more, but I just have to be patient. My mistakes have set me back, and there's a good lesson there, but I won't lecture you. You're a smart girl. Dr. Schwartz tells me I focus too much on what's next, which keeps me from being happy now. I know he's right. He's also trying to help me talk through the accident a little more, but I don't know if I can do that yet. We'll see. He's a good doctor, though, and I'm glad I found him.

Anyway, I'm glad you liked your first week of preschool. (It made me really happy when you took the scarf I gave you for show-and-tell.) I think maybe we'll try the science center again for our mid-week date.

Love, Dad

You take a breath. You read another. And another. And five more. Ten more. You don't know what you expect to find but you're sweating and your hands shake as you read. The dates are sporadic; it seems Graham didn't organize them chronologically, or you're pulling them wrong. It's hard to follow what's going on. There are a few more references to "the accident," and the "mistakes" that seem to have led him into therapy. You have to stop reading. It's too hard to think. You sit back and rub your forehead. *Why is he writing these? To make up for the divorce? Is he really going to give them to her, or is it just some kind of homework from Dr. Schwartz?* If he even still goes to Dr. Schwartz. You haven't seen a letter more recent than two years ago. You frown and look back at the first letter. *Was he still a waiter at Yevgeny's four years ago? He never got promoted?* You look down at the box of letters. There are fifty, maybe sixty more. You have to put them away for now. It's too much to think about and you can't concentrate.

26

You need some air so you grab your backpack and walk cautiously out of the apartment. You won't go far. Somewhere your dad would never go. You get downstairs and walk out into the cool afternoon air. You stop. People are walking by in both directions and there are too many to see each one. They look at the ground, like they're working hard to avoid your eyes. They think you don't notice them, everywhere. You sit on the steps of the apartment building, the hood of your sweatshirt covering your fiery hair. You're not going anywhere.

When you were young, your dad left you alone for four days. It was for a reunion with some of his high school friends in a lodge about an hour away. When he left, you knew he'd be gone overnight, but that was it. You were almost ten, and you were okay with that. You knew how to eat, sleep, and catch the bus by yourself. But he didn't come back. He didn't call. On the third day you wondered if you should call somebody, if maybe there was an accident and he needed help. But if he was fine, if there wasn't an accident and you got him in trouble, that'd be it. So you didn't say anything. But that feeling, that sense of dread, grew inside you. Something terrible was happening, was going to happen, and you had no control. You just had to wait. That fourth night he came home. It was nearly midnight and you had been asleep, so when you heard the door you panicked. You hid under your bed until you heard his familiar subconscious whistling. You were so relieved he wasn't an axe murderer that you went out to the kitchen and hugged him. He seemed happy. He told you about his good time as if you were his wingman, not his daughter. It seems the reunion had turned into a road trip. He'd won a drag race. He'd finally seen the end of *Vertigo*. He'd slept with someone. Things had turned out okay for you, too, but that feeling, the culmination of four days of waiting for some kind of apocalypse, sat in the pit of your stomach. You couldn't let it go.

And now, sitting on the steps with your hood nearly covering your eyes and the whole city against you, that feeling is back. Something bad is happening, is going to happen, and all you can do is sit here and let it. The buzzing in your ears has turned to whispering, and more of the people passing by turn to look at you. *What if he's here? What if he's just waiting for the right moment and I've already lost?*

The sun breaks through the clouds and you shield your eyes with your sleeve. You don't remember why you came out here in the first place so you walk back into the building and climb the stairs to Graham's apartment. You didn't lock the door.

It's 4:06. You walk through the kitchen and remember that you haven't eaten yet. But you just want to sleep. You go into Emerson's room and lie down on the floor. You draw the blankets around you and cover your head with the pillow, but you still can't get rid of the intermittent whispers. You focus on the ticking clock, which gives you some comfort, and eventually fall asleep.

You've never liked falling asleep in the daylight and waking up after dark. It's depressing. You jolt awake after a troubling dream about Britt. You dreamt she drowned in that pond near your apartment complex. She'd been out looking for you, but you weren't there. You shake your head, trying to dispel the image. You look at the clock. 8:35. You're disoriented by the darkness. You thought at first it might be morning.

You go back into Graham's room to make sure you hid his boxes properly. You never did find his liquor.

In the kitchen you find a box of granola. You pour some into a chipped Flintstones bowl and set it on the table. You go to the fridge

Anna

and get the milk and an orange. You eat at the table, wondering when Graham will be home. You think he might have told you this morning, but that was a long time ago.

27

The next few days run together. You don't do much, and you can't make yourself leave the apartment again. Graham's daughter will be over tomorrow.

"What did you tell her about me?" you'd asked him the night before.

"Not a lot. Just that you're a girl who's been a regular at the restaurant and needs a place to stay for a while."

You got up to pile more pasta on your plate. He'd made linguini with pesto sauce.

"What did she say?"

"Not a lot. She doesn't talk much; she'll probably be a little shy around you. But she wanted to know if you like Monopoly."

"Ugh," you groaned, "I fucking hate Monopoly."

"Hey, hey," Graham laughed. "You've got to cut out the language when she's here, all right?" He was attempting a serious tone. "I mean, she's eight. She doesn't watch R-rated movies or frequent truck stops, okay? It's a bad habit, anyway."

You shrugged. "Does she know you smoke? That's a bad habit."

"She knows. I never smoke in the apartment, though." He leaned back. "But you're right. Another bad habit."

You aren't nervous to meet her but you don't want to upset whatever balance they've got. You don't want to be back out on the street.

28

Graham's got another long evening shift, so you go back to the letters. You need to find the first ones to make sense of the rest. The bits of information you've gotten are fragmented, disjointed. Sometimes it's like he forgets he's writing to his daughter, and it's so personal it makes you uncomfortable. You're most interested in the accident—frequently referenced but not yet explained. You know it gives him nightmares. It gives him guilt. And it's never far from his mind. You think maybe he crashed a car and killed somebody, but you've got nothing to go on.

It's hard keeping track of the letters when you've got to keep them in Graham's order. You carefully look through until you find one dated earlier than the others you've read. You feel it's one of the first because it's entirely about the divorce.

11/6/89

Dear Emerson,

I had no idea it would be this hard. It's sad, but I'm glad you're so young; I'm glad you won't remember any of it. We'll make sure we take you to the beach when this is all sorted out and you can start your memories then. I'm still saying "we."

The funny thing is, your mom and I split on good terms. It wasn't a dramatic, vengeful divorce at all. We just weren't happy anymore. And we wanted it to be over. But I didn't realize how huge it was, and how emotional it is to take apart a family like that, until we were in the middle of it.

I guess I'm writing you these letters to help you understand why things ended up the way they did. Maybe so I can understand it, too. And I want you to know who I am, and how much I love you. I know I won't be seeing you as often now, but I will always be here when you need me.

Please know that there is really no one to blame in this situation. Your mom and I are both good people, but I guess when you start out in a doctor/ patient relationship, it's hard not to fall back into those patterns. Anyway, we just ended up being a bad match, and it took us a while to figure that out. And we both love you to pieces. Always.

Love, Dad

You raise your eyebrows. He married his therapist. *Can't imagine why that didn't work out.*

You place the letter back on the others. It seems genuine enough—making a sort of time capsule for Emerson—but there's something unsettling about it as well. As personal as the letters are, he's still hiding. There's so much that's missing. You read a few more. Mostly about the time he spent with her, and little about his past. He mentions New York a few times. He went to culinary school there, had a close group of friends. You know he lost everything, somehow. He left school. Maybe it had to do with the accident. You frown. You feel like you've been through them all. *Where's the first goddamn letter? Why doesn't this make any sense?* It's getting too frustrating for you. You'll have to figure something else out.

29

That night you wait up for Graham. You sit on the couch, trying to read, on edge and scared he's going to know what you've been up to. It makes you jump when you hear his key in the lock.

You've felt guilty about the letters most of the day and that compelled you to do something nice for him, so you cleaned up a little around the apartment and attempted to make a late dinner. You don't know much about cooking, but you were able to manage boiling pasta and heating up sauce.

He walks in, sort of talking to himself, probably assuming you're already asleep, then stops when he sees you in the living room.

"You're up," he says brightly.

"Yeah, I couldn't sleep."

He takes off his shoes and jacket and you slowly stand up, setting aside your book and following him into the kitchen. He laughs when he sees the pots on the stove.

"You're cooking, this late?"

"I didn't know if you get to eat at work . . ." you trail off.

"Oh," he murmurs. "No, I really don't get to eat. This is great, thank you." He pulls down a couple of plates, handing you one.

You sit across from him at the table, your plate piled high with pasta. You're still not used to portion control.

"So, what'd you do today?" Graham asks after a moment.

You think. "I read some," you say slowly. "Slept. Not much, I guess."

"Did you get outside at all?"

You shake your head. "I was outside a couple days ago."

He looks thoughtful. "We should go out tomorrow. Just a walk or something. It's supposed to be nice weather."

"Why?"

He smiles. "It's not good to be stuck in the apartment all the time."

"I don't mind."

His smile turns a little sad, in that pitying way you hate and you want to leave before you hear what you know he's going to say.

"He won't be there," Graham begins gently. "It's been nearly a week since you saw him; he must be long gone by now. And I told you, I won't let anything bad happen."

"You've got tomorrow off?"

"Yeah," he sighs, leaning back in his chair. "Plus the weekend. That's why I've been pulling so many long shifts lately."

You nod, thankful he accepted the change of subject. It's quiet for a minute as you both finish eating, then you stand up hesitantly.

"I think I'm going to go to bed," you say, clearing your plate.

"Sure," he says. "Thanks a lot for the dinner, Laika. It's really just what I needed."

You tell him good night and for some reason it stings to hear him say your name.

30

It's hard for you to fall asleep. There's so much noise in your head, it won't let you rest. You try writing in your journal, but nothing's coming, so you read a bit from it. A few pages of disjointed notes for a story idea. The premise was a group of neighborhood kids go exploring in the woods nearby and find an abandoned shack. Over time they fix it up, make it somewhat livable, and use it as a clubhouse. As an escape. And it makes them lifelong friends. You loved that idea. You were eleven.

A little after one a.m. you finally fall asleep. It's a fitful sleep, though, and it's only an hour before you're up to use the bathroom. You're not used to the apartment at night, so you walk slowly and feel the wall as you go. On the way back into your room you trip over the wooden threshold and fall hard. You stumble back into Emerson's room, cursing. Then you stop.

Someone's there.

You peer hard in the darkness, blinking to make sure it's not a trick of the light. There's a figure sitting on the edge of the bed, looking away from you, out the window. A small figure.

"Who are you?" The figure turns and you see it's a girl. "Are you Emerson?" you ask, moving a little closer. She smiles.

"No. I'm a friend. My name's Hannah."

"How did you get in here?"

"It doesn't matter."

"But you came to see me?"

"I came to help you. I know a lot about you already."

She's wearing pink flannel pajamas and her light hair is in a braid. Her smile is charming. You sit on the bed and lean your back against the headboard.

"I usually sleep on the floor, you know."

"I know."

"Have we met before? I feel like I know you from somewhere."

"I don't think so."

Hannah pulls out a pack of cigarettes from her pocket and you laugh.

"How old are you?"

"Almost ten," she says defensively. She pulls one out and starts to light it.

"Graham doesn't smoke in the house."

She stops. "You really think he tells you everything, don't you?"

"No." You pause. "You think he smokes in the house?"

"I think he likes to make rules."

"It's his place. And it's not like I know him very well."

"But you trust him enough to live here."

"Better than on the street."

Hannah shrugs. "That depends."

"On what?"

"On what he's hiding."

"Are you talking about the letters?"

"I haven't read them." She holds up her cigarette. "Can I light this now, or what?"

"I guess. It doesn't bother me."

"Great."

It's bizarre to see an almost-ten-year-old light up. She crosses her legs on the bed and offers you one.

"No, thanks. It's a bad habit."

"You're a bad habit."

You laugh and she smiles broadly.

"So, why are you sleeping on the floor?" she asks, gesturing to the messy pile of blankets.

"I can't get comfortable here."

"Because it's not your bed?"

"I don't know. It's been a long time since I've slept in a normal room . . . it just doesn't feel right anymore."

She nods. "I prefer the floor, too. But a lot of nights I don't sleep at all."

"At all?"

"Yep."

"Why not?"

"I have a lot on my mind. I talk to people. I have conversations. And I meet people, like you. There's not a lot of time for sleep."

"You talk to people in your head?"

"Sure. Don't you?"

"I hear people whispering sometimes, but I've never talked to them. I think they're watching me, though. I see them staring when I go outside."

"Then you have to be very careful." She sits up a little straighter and looks at you seriously. "Everyone talks. I'm sure they're just waiting for you to make a mistake."

"You think my dad has talked to them?"

"He's already in the city, right?"

"Yeah."

"Then I'll bet he has. You can't trust anybody."

You look out the window, letting her words sink in. You need to be more careful. Hannah looks at her watch.

"It's late. I'd better go."

"Okay. Will you be back?"

"Whenever I can."

She gets up and heads toward the door. "Don't worry, I'm going to help you."

You nod and she slips out of the room. You sink into your blankets and fall asleep in no time.

31

The kitchen table is cleared except for the game board and you're sitting stiffly in your chair, tapping the pewter battleship against the wood. Emerson is taking forever. Graham's been giving you appreciative glances, but you're not sure how to think of him since Hannah's visit, and you just want to get back to the letters and figure this out.

"All right; I'll take it," Emerson says finally, handing Graham the money for St. Charles Place.

"Good," Graham says, smiling at you. "Your turn, Laika."

You roll the dice. You land on one of Emerson's properties and she laughs. It startles you. She collects your money—she has most of your money—but then you see she's drawing something on a scrap of paper and after a minute she hands it to you.

"I don't want you to run out," she says. The paper has dollar signs and stars all over it with your name at the top, spelled "Lyka."

"Thanks."

You know she means she doesn't want the game to be over, but it was still nice, you suppose. You've decided you like her, even though she seems a little strange. She keeps checking the rules obsessively, making sure everyone's following, but she must have played this game a thousand times and you thought she'd have them memorized. She was patient with you, though, helping you remember how to play since it had been a few years, and she didn't seem nervous to have you there. She said she liked your hair and she liked your name.

But you feel like it's been a couple of hours and you've almost had enough. Graham looks wilted himself, and when Emerson says she's going to the bathroom, he stands as well.

"All right, Em," he says, "I'm going downstairs for a minute. And pretty soon I'll have to start cheating, okay?"

"But it's not the third hour."

"It's close," he smiles. "And it's nearly bedtime."

She starts saying something about the rules again but then turns and walks down the hall and you can't hear her anymore.

"Come down with me," Graham says to you, nodding toward the door. "We'll get some air."

You nod. He doesn't want you to be alone with her.

You walk down the steps with him and out the door to the front of the complex. The air is still and cool and it does make you feel better.

"You having a good time?" he asks after a moment.

"Monopoly?"

"No," he laughs, "I know that game is hell. Sorry about that. I just meant with Emerson."

"She seems nice."

Graham pulls out his cigarettes and you can tell he's happy you said that.

"I think she likes you. I haven't seen her talk this much in a while."

You nod.

Graham takes a breath and he looks down at his hands, his smile fading. He's holding his matches and a lighter, but he's not doing anything. He puts the matchbook away and you wonder if he's thinking about quitting. But the lighter's still in his hand and he gently rolls his thumb over the spark wheel and you see he's starting to shake. He blinks hard and looks at you uncertainly.

"You trying to quit, or something?" you ask, frowning. You don't know what he's doing and it's making you nervous.

He shakes his head. "No." Then he holds the lighter out to you. "Can you light it for me?"

"Why?"

"Sometimes I can't. I've got this thing . . . I'm sorry."

You take the lighter cautiously and click it on. He holds the cigarette to the flame and you can see he's trying to keep it together.

"Sorry." He breathes the smoke in deeply. "I don't know what my problem is."

You look up at the apartment, suddenly wishing you weren't alone with him.

32

Emerson didn't mind giving up her room. You thought it would be hard for her since she seems to like a certain routine, but now she's more interested in showing you all her stuff.

"Do you like animals?" she asks, digging a few stuffed toys and a doctor kit out of her closet. "I want to be a veterinarian."

You shrug. "I guess."

"Here," she says, handing you a gray cat. "We can give them a check-up."

She brings out the rest of the animals and carefully lines them up, but then starts muttering to herself about missing one. She goes back through the closet, shoving toys and clothes aside, and she seems to be getting upset about it.

"Did you see the horse? It's brown with a white spot and it goes right here." She points to a vacant place between the black dog and the purple elephant.

You shake your head.

She goes out the door, muttering again. You put the cat in the empty spot and look under the bed, just in case it got shoved under there.

A minute later she comes back with the horse, smiling.

"Okay," she sighs, "now—No, no," she interrupts herself, looking down at the cat. She picks it up and moves it to the end of the line, then sets the horse in its proper place. "This is how they go."

You nod. "Sorry."

"It's okay," she says good-naturedly, "I'll show you."

She shows you her toys for another twenty minutes or so, until Graham tells her it's time for bed. She finishes the animal check-up and says they all have names that start with "W." She rattles them off but you can't remember more than two or three. She brings out her rock collection and tells you where they all came from. She's naming these places around her apartment and Graham's apartment and her school, and you start to get an uneasy feeling and her voice is getting drowned out by the whispers rising in your ears. You look around and expect to see Hannah or at least something unusual, but it's only Graham in the doorway.

You both get up and you say good night and Emerson she says she'll tell you more about it in the morning, but you just want to cover your ears because the static in your head is getting so loud. You think Graham knows something is wrong because he's watching you carefully, but you can't think about anything right now. You just want to sleep. You'll worry about it tomorrow.

33

You're going to figure this out. You think you've read all the letters but there's so much missing, you must have made a mistake. Graham's working lunch today so after you wake up, you slip into his room, unlock the file cabinet, and unearth the box. You open the lid. There they are—still nicely folded in an infuriatingly pointless order. You hesitate for just a moment,

He will kill me

then you dump them out. You hear the buzzing. Then the whispers. Then Hannah's voice forces its way into your head.

He's out there now. Talking to them.

You cover your ears to make them stop. You smack your head and bury your face and they start to fade. You just have to focus. You start unfolding the letters and organizing them by date. You read over them as you go, but they're still hard to follow.

You hear a noise behind you. A creak.

You spin around, your heart slamming. You push your hair out of your eyes.

"Hannah? Jesus, you scared the shit out of me."

"Sorry." She stands nonchalantly in the doorway. "I thought you might be doing something stupid, so I came over. Looks like I was right."

"What are you talking about? You said I had to figure out what he's hiding."

She shakes her head like an annoyed parent. "You're not going to find anything in there. He's too smart for that."

You turn toward the letters. "But I'm putting them in order. If I find the first one—" You turn back around but she's gone.

"Fine," you mutter. "That's fine."

You go back to work, arranging the dates, skimming the letters for significant details. You feel lost in a maze. It seems like there are more letters than there were a few days ago, but there are some you can't find that you know you've already read. You rub your forehead. Another creak and a footstep behind you. *Leave me alone.* You roll your eyes and turn around to tell Hannah to get lost, but it's not Hannah. You scramble to your feet.

"What's going on here?"

Graham is standing at the door with his tie in one hand and confused, reddened eyes.

You want to say something but you can't think in a straight line. He's looking around, putting it together. His eyes turn harsh.

"I can't believe this." His voice is rising. "You went through my room?"

"I'm sorry."

There's yelling in your head now, and you stare at the floor. Graham throws down his tie and storms in.

"That's not fucking good enough."

You take a step back. He's thrown you off. It's strange to see him this way. You haven't seen him really angry before, even with that asshole, Jack. You know now that Hannah was right: you did something stupid. And you lost track of time.

"I just wanted to know what's going on."

"What does that mean?"

"I don't know . . . I guess I mean, I mean about you. I don't really know you. I wanted to make sure I—"

"By reading my private thoughts to my daughter?"

He seems to be ramping up. He's starting to sweat.

"I don't know."

He takes a breath, closing his eyes. *This is where he'll lose it.* You watch him carefully.

"What is it you think of me?" he asks finally. "That I'm some kind of a sicko?"

You waver slightly. You don't say anything.

"Then maybe you shouldn't even be here," he mutters. "Maybe you'd be better off . . ."

He pauses and looks down like he's trying to compose himself.

"What?" you demand, already sure where he's going with it and unable to suppress your attitude. "Tell me."

"Never mind."

"Back on the street, right?" you press, daring him to admit it. "Maybe back with my dad?" You're walking a line but you feel like yourself again and you never were any good at keeping quiet.

"I didn't say that. But this . . ." He glowers at the letters. "You went too far."

"Well, what am I supposed to do?" you shoot back angrily. "Believe whatever you say? I'm just trying to figure out what kind of person I'm living with."

He rubs the side of his face and you see his hand is trembling. You've made it worse, but you don't care. When he speaks it's practically in a growl.

"This was none of your business. You shouldn't have been in here."

"Then what am I supposed to do?" you repeat, nearly shouting. "You tell me this is safe, right? That you're a good guy. Well, fantastic. Am I just supposed to hang out while you hide your drugs and your alcohol and your fucking murder weapons in the next room?" You laugh scornfully. "I guess you're just used to people doing whatever you tell them. That's a pretty good d—"

He slams the side of his fist into the wall and you jump. You stop talking.

He will

You take another step back.

kill me.

"It was none of your business," he repeats in a low voice.

"You're right," you mumble, wondering why the hell you wanted to test him in the first place. "You're right."

He moves toward you and his face is dark. You've pushed him too far. You think about running but there's no way out. He comes closer and you wince and close your eyes and squeeze your fists to brace yourself for whatever's coming. You wait. You open your eyes and he's just standing in front of you, looking worn. You're waiting and your palms sweat and your adrenaline rushes and you're getting mad because he's just doing this to fuck with you. *Why won't he just get it over with?* You can't read his face anymore.

"What?" you finally cry. "What are you waiting for?"

He's silent.

"Am I supposed to pick one of these?" You grab one of his belts from the closet shelf and toss it to him. "Is that how it works?"

He looks down at his hands and you think maybe you've made things worse for yourself again, but then he lets the belt drop.

"No," he says. "No, I'm not going to do that." He frowns again at the letters strewn over the floor. "But I do want to be alone now."

Back on the street.

"Okay," you say, still watching him distrustfully.

He's not looking at you anymore. You move out of the room as quietly as you can, as if a sudden noise would break the spell and change his mind.

34

You go back to Emerson's room and close the door softly. You sit on the bed and rest your head on your knees as the noise level in your mind rises. You're so tired of listening. You start to cry. After a moment you hear a squeaking sound and raise your head to see Hannah standing at the window, writing against the glass with her finger.

"I didn't want to bother you," she says softly. "I was leaving you a note."

You peer at the window. It says, "Get smart, dumbass."

"What did I do now?" you ask, wiping your eyes with your sleeve.

"You tell me," she replies, sitting again at the foot of the bed. "You're the one getting yelled at and crying."

"I shouldn't have read the letters."

She laughs. "The letters don't mean a damn thing. Do you really think he'd put anything important somewhere you could find it?"

"Then why did he get so mad?"

"Because you're looking. You're onto him and it's only a matter of time before you figure out his secret."

"What's his secret?"

"You want me to tell you? That's not much fun."

"Hannah, tell me."

"Fine. I only just found out, myself." She pauses. "He's working for Casey Ephrem."

Your stomach sinks.

"How do you know that?" you whisper.

"See, you're being stupid again," she snaps. "You need to focus. You know those people you hear? I can hear them, too, except they're not whispering. If you pay attention, things start to make sense. They'll tell you things."

"The people watching me—they told you? Does Graham talk to them, too?"

She nods. "Remember, everybody talks. But think about it: you see your dad on the street and the same day Graham offers you a place to stay. Casey's recruited him to get information about you. To find out what you've been doing since you left—and who you've talked to."

You start shaking. You were right; they're all watching you, all trying to send you back. Trying to get you killed.

"What do I do? I can't stay here, right? I've got to leave." You make a move to get up but Hannah stops you.

"That would be a mistake."

"Why?"

"You leave now, and all those people on the outside will move in on you. You've got to pretend everything's okay. Make up with Graham, but don't give him any more information. You'll need a real plan before you can get out."

"He might kick me out, though. He's really mad."

She shakes her head. "He won't. He'll try to fix things between you, tell you lies, get you to believe him again." She looks at you hard. "Don't believe him."

You nod.

You actually feel better. All the things you suspected, everything you saw and heard and felt was right. They are against you, and Graham's the worst of them all. He and your dad were probably in league from the first day you stumbled upon Yevgeny Alekseev's.

"I should go," Hannah says, slipping off the bed. "Just remember to pay attention, all right? You'll never make it if you don't."

"Yeah. See you around."

35

After Hannah leaves, you climb off the bed and pull the comforter tight over the mattress again. You sit on the floor, trying to think of what to do. You glance under the bed at your journal. You take it to the bookshelf and pull a few books forward, sliding your journal behind them until it's completely obscured. Maybe you should destroy it after all. It would give him everything.

You sit back down on the floor and think of what you'll say. How you should play this. He's dangerous and you have to be careful.

You hold your head and wish you'd run away north or east. Maybe you should have just tried to stay until you turned eighteen. Maybe you should have bought that gun.

There's a knock at the door and you get to your feet and you're nervous but you tell him to come in.

Graham smiles faintly when he enters the room, but his eyes are still red and he looks a little sick.

"I'm sorry," you say quickly. You know your eyes are red now, too. "I shouldn't have gone through your stuff. I just . . ."

You don't know how to finish. He sits down on the floor, so you sit, too.

"I know. I'm sorry I got so upset," he says. "And I would never try to send you back with Casey, or make you leave."

tell you lies

"It's okay."

"I know it's hard to believe I'm helping you just to be nice. I know that's not what you're used to." He sighs. "And I really do understand wanting a little background on the guy you live with. I think I owe you that. I can tell you now, whatever you want to know, but it really just amounts to the fact that I've had rough patches in my life, and I've dealt with some better than others. But I promise you, there is nothing scary or terrible that I've done."

You nod but don't meet his eyes. *He would kill me if he knew.* You wonder what part Emerson has in all this. If she's in danger, too.

"Tell me about the accident," you say suddenly.

The people from the street take over again, whispering fiercely to each other, and you shake your head but Hannah's voice explodes into your mind, overpowering them. *Do you want to do this alone?* she shouts. *I told you to play it cool, not give him more reason to suspect you. You're hopeless.*

"Are you okay?" you faintly hear Graham ask.

You lift your head up from where it had been buried in your hands.

"Yeah," you manage to reply. "What did I say?"

"You wanted to know about the accident."

"Did you already tell me?"

"No . . ." He frowns. "Are you sure you're okay?"

"I'm fine."

"Okay. I will tell you, if you want to know."

You nod and hope they stay out of your head for a goddamn minute so you can listen.

"All right," he says, taking a breath and leaning back against the bed frame. "I was a few years older than you—eighteen, I guess, because I'd just finished high school. I wasn't planning on college, so I used my savings to take a trip. I spoke a little German, so I decided on Frankfurt."

His voice is wobbly and you see something about him is different, and you almost regret asking him to do this. Then you remember; he's not feeling anything. It's an act and your dad is stage manager. He's never been to Frankfurt.

"Anyway," he says, "I stayed in cheap hostels and mainly traveled around to neighboring towns. One weekend, though, I decided to take the overnight train to Lübeck. It was crowded and noisy but I still fell asleep pretty fast. An hour or so later I woke up to this horrible sound. Metal tearing apart. I thought a bomb had gone off. Then I was thrown to the ground and lost consciousness, but only for a few minutes, I think. When I woke up, the train was on fire. Not my car, which was at the back, but the three ahead of mine. I got out with the others and tried to help people out of the other cars, but . . ." he shakes his head. "Everyone was on fire, and everyone was screaming. I wasn't any help at all. I just kept throwing up."

Graham adjusts his position and you think maybe he wants to stop, but he doesn't.

"We learned later it was rail damage," he continues. "The tracks hadn't been maintained and were starting to crack. Sixty-seven people died. And I felt I should have been one of them." He blinks hard, like something hurts.

And when he speaks again you feel like he's talking to himself. "I carried that with me, and it really fucked me up for a while. I did try college then, but failed out. I couldn't hold down a job, I didn't leave my apartment for months. I didn't want to do anything or talk to anyone, so most of the time I didn't. I saw a few doctors, but it still took me over ten years to pull myself out of it." He pauses. "I don't know, though. Maybe I can't ever really pull myself out of it."

You're watching him, but all you can hear is the clock ticking. It used to be soothing to you—a soft constant for your mind to focus on—but now it's harsh and loud. It's trying to tell you something. You stare at it, thinking. You know you're being stupid, you don't need Hannah to tell you, but you want to figure it out before she does.

"You'll never figure it out," Graham says.

You jolt back to the room, turning toward him with pounding temples.

"What?" you manage to ask.

"You will never figure it out," he says again with careful enunciation.

The people from the street are screaming at each other now, like some kind of alarm has been sounded but they can't calm down enough to follow the protocol. Hannah's screaming at you again, too, but you can't listen to her now. You bury your head in your hands and beg them to go away, just for a little while, until you can deal with Graham.

Graham.

You raise your head and see he's standing over you. You rush to your feet and back up until you're touching the wall. In a final attempt to dispel the voices, you shake your head fiercely and they die down a bit.

"Can you hear me? Are you okay?" he's saying. You just watch. He's very close to you now, looking into your eyes.

"Are you okay?" he repeats. He touches your shoulder and you push him back, crying out.

"I will figure it out!" you shout. "I know what you're doing!"

They explode again.

"What?" Graham asks, feigning confusion. "What do you mean?"

"The clocks!" you say triumphantly, hoping your knowledge of his plans scares the shit out of him. "I know you're using the clocks."

"The clocks?" He frowns, glancing up at the one on the wall. "I'm sorry, I really . . . I don't know what you're saying. I think you might be having a dream."

Good one.

"I don't need you to help me out," you assure him, leaning against the wall. "I'm listening now; I can hear everything." You pause for a moment and let the volume in your head rise again. The clock sets a rhythm for the conversation. It's loud but it's starting to make sense. You laugh. "I don't need your help."

"You think Hannah will take care of you?"

You flinch. "You know about Hannah?"

"I know about everything," he murmurs, gesturing toward the clock. "You're in way over your head."

You shake your head and concentrate hard on what the people on the street are saying. Graham's still talking but his voice is fading. Soon you can't hear him at all.

He'll give us orders soon. I'll signal you when it's time, you hear one of them say. The other answers back with a slight laugh, *I'll be ready.* You can separate their voices now, and they're no longer whispers. Hannah was right. You just have to pay attention.

"Hey."

You look up to see Hannah in the doorway, behind Graham. She's shaking her head.

"You need to get rid of him."

"Why?"

"We need to talk."

"I'm right, aren't I?"

"Just get rid of him," she says evenly.

You look at Graham and he's watching you closely. You rub your eyes.

"I'm tired," you say flatly. "Can I go to bed?"

"Right now?"

You nod, already walking over to your blankets and lying down.

"You don't want dinner?"

"No."

You close your eyes. But he's still there.

"Do you feel all right?" he asks after a few seconds. "You might be getting sick."

"No. I'm not."

You don't open your eyes and after a few more seconds you hear him turn around to leave.

"Okay, but let me know if you need something. Good night," he says faintly as he closes the door.

36

You keep your eyes closed for a few minutes until you hear Hannah. She's rustling paper. You open your eyes. She's up on the bed, reading a book.

"You're reading?" you ask, surprised.

"That's right." She turns a page without looking at you.

"Now?"

"Clearly, you don't need me."

"What are you talking about?"

She closes the book and turns to you. "All you had to do was keep quiet with Graham. You couldn't even do that."

"I had to scare him," you retort. "He needs to know I'm not going to let him win—that I can play at his level."

"You can't play at his level!" she shouts, throwing down her book. "You'll get yourself killed."

You shake your head, not wanting to believe it.

"Casey's in charge," Hannah continues. "Do you think he'll hesitate? Do you think any of them will?" She gestures toward the street.

"I was right about the clocks, wasn't I?"

"What about the clocks?"

"I think he's using them to spy on me. You know, to gather information."

She shrugs. "Probably."

"So . . ."

"So, you need to stop giving yourself away," she snaps. "You tell him you know about the clocks, and he'll just do something else. You're not going to scare him. You're going to get yourself killed."

You look out the window. It might be raining. Looks a little like snow. You didn't think there was snow here. And it seems early, but you can't remember what month it is.

"So, what do I do?"

"Stop being so stupid," Hannah replies gravely. "Fix this with Graham. You won't get another chance if you fuck up again. He thought you might be dreaming, so convince him you were." She gets up. "Maybe you are getting sick."

You nod. "All right. I'll do it."

"Good." She starts to walk toward the door.

"I hear them better now," you say. "The people on the street, I mean. You were right; when I started listening they stopped whispering."

She nods. "You can use them. They don't know you can hear."

"One of them said they're getting orders soon. There'll be some kind of a signal. Do you know what that means?"

"It means fix this thing with Graham before he reports back to your dad."

She walks out the door, and you're left with the deafening ticking

maybe you are getting sick

of the clock. You take it off the wall and wrap it in a towel, then shove it under the bed.

Chapter 37

Graham

It's the Way We Carry It

The cigarette in his hand shook as Graham leaned against the wall. He couldn't even use a lighter anymore. He'd gotten Carl, one of the young waiters, to light it for him before he'd finished his break and gone back inside. Now Graham was alone and couldn't seem to relax, even with his cigarette and brief solitude. This time it had been three nights since he'd slept.

"Graham, we'll need you back in five," called Wendy, turning back to the kitchen and letting the door swing shut before he could respond.

That's fine, he thought, resting the back of his head against the brick wall and closing his eyes. They were cutting his breaks in half that night, but there was really no way around it when the place got busy. He wished he could take a few days off, just to be there with Laika and work on building back the trust he'd lost, but Yevgeny's was still understaffed and he needed the money. Graham shook his head.

He'd been an asshole before, overreacting and losing his temper like that with her. Sure, going through his stuff was a violation that caught him completely off guard, but it made perfect sense. Graham was a stranger. He would have wanted Emerson to do the same thing. But she thought he would hurt her. She was ready for it, like it was only a matter of time before he took out some kind of frustration on her. And that really tore him up. He thought now maybe he just had some kind of threatening way about him—a toxic vibe he emitted that made people think he was up to no good.

Graham wasn't sure what time it was, but knew his five minutes were up. He ground the rest of his cigarette under his shoe. A few feet over he could still see the black mark from his match failure months ago. He sighed heavily. He needed to call Anna. It'd be late when he got off, but he might try anyway. He needed advice about Laika, about whatever she was going through.

He was pretty sure she was seeing things the other day, when she started yelling about clocks and then got that odd, vacant stare. She wasn't with him at all. Graham knew a little about it; he'd had experience with hallucinations to the point where he'd been medicated a few times. One night, nearly two years ago, he was walking home from work and saw a city bus crash in the distance. He saw it overturn, and heard the screeching brakes and the powerful boom of metal hitting pavement. He started yelling and running toward it, calling for people around him to come help, but nobody moved. People on the sidewalk stared at him oddly and he felt like he was in one of his nightmares. Running toward wreckage. But when he got closer, he saw the bus was still upright and undamaged, idling at the bus stop. He looked around frantically, slowly coming to understand the crash had only existed in his mind.

That scared him badly. He'd sat on the curb for a long time and thought about keeping it to himself, worried a doctor or lawyer or police officer would try to take away his custody of Emerson. It's a terrible feeling, not knowing what's real. He couldn't trust himself.

"Graham! Now!" Jack shouted from the door.

Graham blinked a few times to bring himself back, then walked over to Jack.

"Sorry."

"You're taking Bina's tables, too. She just went home sick."

"Is she all right?"

"Christ, I couldn't give a fuck," Jack replied, annoyed. "Just get in there."

Graham walked in and tried to reorient himself. He didn't remember his own tables. If he got through this shift it would be a miracle. And he needed to sleep tonight. Whatever happened, he needed to sleep. He stood at the entrance to the main dining room for a moment, unsure of what to do next.

"Table twelve," Carl said gently, suddenly beside him. "They've been here the longest. Bina got their drinks but didn't take their orders."

Graham smiled at him. "Thanks."

He moved toward the table, glancing at its occupants. Three couples, late-fifties. They didn't seem bothered by the wait.

"I'm sorry," he began, "Bina had to leave, so I'll be taking care of you. My name's Graham."

He pulled his notepad out of his shirt pocket, but dropped the pen. He bent down to pick it up and was overcome by a feeling of vertigo, and his vision darkened. He stood slowly, taking a few calculated breaths and praying it resolved.

"Are you all right, son?" one of the men asked. Graham looked up and saw they were all watching him. "You don't look well."

"Oh, I'm fine," he assured them. "Thank you."

Regulars could have told them Graham looked like that pretty much all the time, but he was still disheartened to know it took strangers less than a minute to realize he was a wreck. He did his best to concentrate while he wrote down their orders, but most of his focus was spent on steadying his hands. He took the ticket to the window and grabbed the bottle of horseradish a different table had asked him for. He glanced at the clock over the kitchen.

I know you're using the clocks.

He still had three hours to go. Graham turned to face the room but couldn't remember which table had just asked him for the horseradish. *Why does she think I'm part of this?* He frowned, wondering what Laika was up to at his place. He always took the file cabinet key with him now, so he knew she wasn't reading the letters, but if she was seeing things again, she could end up hurting herself. And he was obviously a sinister character in her hallucination, if that's even what it was. Graham's stomach sank as he realized he'd lost even more trust.

Then he fell. He tripped over the edge of the carpet and lost his grip on the horseradish, which shot across the floor and cracked open as it hit the wall. The restaurant was crowded so nobody seemed to notice, but after Graham picked up the fragmented bottle he turned to see Jack behind him.

"In the kitchen," he growled. Graham looked toward the front door, thinking maybe he should save time and just leave. "Now, Calley."

Graham followed him back and they stopped just under the exit sign and Jack had his hand over his mouth like he was summoning all his patience before he spoke.

"First of all, you've lost Bina's tables, and her tips, all right? I'm giving them to Andrei."

Graham nodded. He dumped the remains of the horseradish jar into the trash can next to him and wiped his hands on his apron. Jack's prominent temple vein was throbbing and Graham wondered how he could handle the stress of this business. He was maybe fifty-five, with a tall, intimidating build and such an explosive personality it was no wonder he'd never married. The only one from the restaurant who could stand him was his best friend, Vlad, the owner who'd hired him as manager.

"I'm sorry, Jack; I know I've been off tonight."

"You're off every night! You've made mistakes on three orders, completely forgotten two of your tables, and that jar was the second thing you've broken on your shift."

"It's been a hard couple of weeks for me," Graham muttered, ashamed to use his personal life as an excuse. "I'll turn it around."

"Listen," Jack said in a tone so uncharacteristically calm that it made Graham take a wary step back, "I know you want to be line cook. But there's no fucking way you'll survive the back of the house if you can't work the front. You get it?"

"Yeah. I get it."

"I'm putting you on official probation. I know we're short-staffed and everything, but I will not hesitate to fire you if you fuck up again."

"I know. Thanks, Jack."

"You should have a real manageable load out there now. Just four two-tops. So keep your head in the game and sort out your shit on your own time."

Graham nodded and returned to the front. It killed him to admit it, but Jack was right; he was to blame for being stuck in the job he hated. Jack might have been an asshole, but he wasn't the one stalling Graham's career. He sighed, but forced himself to push it away and get back to work. He'd be home soon enough.

38

He bought it, you think. You told him you felt off, that you hadn't slept well for a few nights when in reality you'd been sleeping fifteen or sixteen hours each day. You told him you thought you might be getting your first period. Hannah liked that. You made him uncomfortable enough to drop it, and you think he was convinced. He knows you've been through a lot.

You take down all the clocks while he's at work. You wrap them in blankets or towels or sweatshirts so you don't hear the ticking. You put them all back before he gets home. You don't think about his letters anymore. Hannah's right: they're meaningless. Instead you scour the apartment for clues, which turn out to be everywhere. He moves his cigarettes between the left and right sides of the bookcase. He changes the order of the videos in the cabinet. He places grains of salt on top of certain boxes of cereal in the pantry. He's communicating this way. He's giving out information to your dad, to the people on the street.

The phone rings and you jump. You look at it. *Why not?*

"Hello?"

"Hi . . . is this Anna?"

You glance at the fridge.

"No."

"Oh, Emerson. Sorry. This is Walt. Remember me? Your dad's friend."

"Okay."

"Can you just let him know I called? He's got my number."

"Sure."

"Great. Thanks a lot."

Walt. You go write his name down in your journal. You don't plan on giving Graham the message but you don't want to forget the name. He could be important.

39

That night Graham makes lasagna. He has to wake you up again.

"You doing okay?" he asks across the table.

You nod. "I've been getting more sleep," you smile. "I do feel better. Thanks."

"I think we should try looking for your aunt soon."

"How?"

"We'll get out the map, call information, and just try a bunch of cities." He leans over to pick up the napkin he dropped on the floor. "We'll start here and move outward. What do you think?"

"Sure." You'd managed to forget about her these last couple of weeks.

You watch him closely when he looks away, wondering what he wants with your aunt. She might have a part in all this.

You force yourself to eat and smile and answer his questions, but everywhere you look there's more proof you're not safe. He's been moving the tea-kettle. Counterclockwise, from burner to burner. And the lasagna is making you queasy. You rub your forehead.

"How was work?" you ask.

"Good," he says brightly. "I only got yelled at once."

"What'd you do?"

He shrugs. "Dropped a tray. The dishes were empty, though."

"That's great."

You wonder if he moves it while you're sleeping. You need to stop sleeping so much. He takes a bite and looks up at you.

"So, you're keeping busy? Reading some books?"

"Yeah," you say slowly. "Pretty much." He's watching you intently, like there's something he's looking for.

"You get outside at all?"

He wants to know if I'm talking to anyone.

"No."

"Have you . . . gotten to take a shower, or anything?"

He looks uncomfortable. You're not sure what he's getting at until you realize it's probably been two weeks since you showered. You haven't really thought about it.

"I will tonight," you say, looking down at your grungy clothes.

He smiles and you take another bite of lasagna but now you're convinced it tastes odd. Chalky. And it's making your stomach pitch. You stop and take a breath.

"You sure you're okay?" he asks. He takes a long drink of water.

You look around the room, trying to think, and pushing away the conversations growing in your head. You can't listen now, not while you're focused on Graham.

You feel the veins in your wrists jolt. You look down at your plate.

It's him.

You tell him you know about the clocks,
and he'll just do something else.

He put something in your food.

"Yeah," you say, trying to keep calm. "I think I'll go take a shower now."

"Okay." He's frowning and you wonder if he already knows you've figured it out. "I was thinking we might want to get you a check-up soon. Just let a doctor make sure everything looks good, you know? Since you've been on your own."

You're not sure what he's doing with this. But you're sure your dad put him up to it, and there's no way you're seeing a doctor with him. You smile a little, though, because you have to play along, and you can't afford to make any more mistakes.

"Okay."

You can't think about that now, though. You look down at your plate again and wonder what it is he puts in there. Something to get information out of you, or maybe just poison to kill you, you don't know.

You stand up and carefully turn toward the bathroom.

"If you want, we can watch a movie when you're done," he says.

You look at him and he seems so casual, like all of this is so effortless for him, and you feel a wave of hatred rush over you. He wouldn't think twice about killing you. Maybe it's already done.

"Sure."

You didn't die. You lay awake all night, waiting for it, but nothing happened. So now you know it was something else, something that's inside you now. You think about it until you realize

I'll signal, I'll be ready, I'll signal you when

he's trying to hear what you hear. He's slipping something into your food that will let him read your thoughts and listen to the conversations. He can hear the people on the street. He can hear Hannah. You don't know how to control them or stop your thoughts, so there's nothing you can do. Except stop eating.

40

It's 1:08 p.m. Graham just left for the restaurant so you can finally make a plan. You dig in your backpack for something you haven't looked at in a long time: your map of the city. You think about Mark's Deli, Parker Grocery, Northside Diner, one of the old places. You're not sure if you can still do it. You haven't been outside in weeks.

Your hair is so matted you can't brush the tangles out. You put it up and decide it doesn't matter.

Outside the air is still. People are looking at you, like always, but you're not going to listen to them yet. You need to focus on your plan. It's a short walk to Jessman's, a big chain grocery store on the west side that you hate because it's so bright and dirty and always crowded. But you've been out of it for so long, you need a sure thing.

You walk west on Sixty-First until you get to Coal Ridge Road. Jessman's is right on the corner and the parking lot is full, as usual. A few men, professional types, watch you as you approach, then glance at their watches and walk into the store. A young couple does the same thing. The woman taps her watch. *I have to. I have to eat.* You shake your head and walk in. You'll change your strategy, though; with all these people watching you, you feel too conspicuous. You pull out a cart and push it inside. You set your backpack in the front and start putting things in the basket. You've got to make this look real.

The first empty aisle you're in is the cereal row. You toss a few granola bars in the cart and slip a few more into your backpack. You do the same thing with cheese, peanut butter, bagels, instant coffee. Graham commented on how much coffee you drink—he said it's a wonder you're not up all night. But that just means he's done something to it as well, because you sleep more than ever. You need your own. You can't trust anything in that apartment.

You push your cart back up the aisles to the front of the store. The canned goods. You park it in the middle of the row and walk toward the door with your backpack on, scanning the cans carefully. You force yourself to walk slowly. As soon as everyone's gone and you feel it's safe, you walk out the door.

It worked. You can't believe it worked. You walk back down Sixty-First and you're filled with a rush of emotion you haven't felt in months. Maybe years.

Then you notice them.

You hear them before you see them.

This is Forty-Five. I've got Devushka.

Same, Forty-Five. East on Sixty-First.

Move in?

Seriously? Who said that?

Easy, Nine. No orders, no movement. You know that.

They're talking about you. They're using Russian now. They're making fun of you, making fun of your mother. He must have told them to do that.

You look around and see what you always see: too many people, too many faces. They stare at you openly, like they don't even care what you know. Maybe they don't.

No word, no word. Check.

An older man checks his watch as he crosses in front of you. Two college-age guys tap theirs as they pass each other.

You frown and slow your pace. The watches.

Coming up on you, Twenty-Eight.

That's how they signal each other.

You should have been paying attention; you would have noticed it earlier. You spent so much time ignoring them, hoping they would stop staring, stop talking, stop whispering, that you didn't realize you could learn from them. Until Hannah.

Why Friday? He told me Tuesday.

Jesus, plans change, Thirty-Three. Let it go.

We need to meet. We have options, you know.

No. He doesn't want an accident, okay?

Moving east.

I think that's north now, Twelve.

Will you tell the lowers to shut up? I can't fucking think!

They're beginning to sound frantic. You need to get back to the apartment.

You start to run because they know your location and maybe you could lose them. You take the back streets and nearly get lost trying to throw them off. But you make it.

You stumble up the stairs. You're wheezing and need both hands to guide your key into the door. You slam it shut and lock it behind you, carrying your backpack into Emerson's room. The fleeting sense of victory you felt outside Jessman's is completely gone. That must have been part of the plan, too.

41

After a few more of Emerson's visits, she only wants to play with you. You don't really understand it; you're not that good with kids and she ends up doing most of the talking, but she seeks you out anyway. Last time her mom came—Anna—and you're sure she's worried about you staying there, what you might do and say and how you're a dangerous influence on her daughter, but it's Graham she should be worried about.

"This game is awesome," Emerson breathes as you shuffle the cards for another round. Graham is making dinner in the kitchen and her door's open so you can hear the occasional clanging of pots and murmurs as he reads himself the recipe.

"Your dad never taught you Speed?"

She shakes her head. "He doesn't really like card games."

"But he likes Monopoly?"

"Everybody likes Monopoly."

"Okay."

You play a few more rounds before you remember what you wanted to show her.

Did the plan change?

. . . No.

What are you talking about, Seventeen?

The other target. Is there another target?

I swear to God—

No, Seventeen. Just the one target.

You do your best to ignore them as you pull the drawings out from under your blanket. You need a break. You bring the pages over to Emerson. You ripped them out of your journal before she got there, so you wouldn't have to show her the whole thing.

"I drew these when I was eight," you say. "I know you like animals, so . . ." You hand her the pages.

She looks through them carefully.

"You drew this?" she asks, looking at the one of birds flying over the ocean, done in oil pastel. You nod. "It's good," she says.

The other one she likes is of a dog you once saw on the street, sleeping outside a bar. You did that in colored pencil, using up most of your brown and black ones. She hands them back and says she wishes she could draw. It's nice she's impressed but you know they aren't very good. Things look different when you're eight, though.

"I'm sure you can draw," you say.

"Nope," Emerson replies matter-of-factly. "I don't really like to, though."

"What do you like?"

"Math, I guess." She's putting the cards in order as she talks. "I'm good at that." You nod. "Really anything but social studies," she laughs. "I got a quiz back the other day and I missed all the answers."

You hear a loud noise from the kitchen—a dropped pan or slammed cabinet—and it startles you. You look back at Emerson, but she doesn't seem to have heard it. Your heartbeat quickens.

"You missed all the answers?" you repeat.

"Yep."

"Was Graham mad?"

"Not really. He said we'll have to study more next time."

"He didn't yell?"

She looks up, like she's thinking about it. "He doesn't yell much."

"Then what does he do?"

"What do you mean?"

"When he's mad, what does he do?" You're watching her closely now.

"He gets quiet. And he takes stuff away—TV, games, that kind of thing."

"Does he ever leave you alone?"

"Like, in the apartment?" You nod. "No," she says, looking puzzled. "I'm not old enough."

You smile and hope she's right. You hope she's safe and that she's not part of this plan your dad and Graham are running. You hope they know when to stop.

42

The phone rings. It wakes you up, actually. You dig the clock out from under the bed and see that it's nearly eight p.m. Graham's supposed to be home but the phone keeps ringing. You get up.

In the kitchen you find a note that says he's closing for somebody who called in sick. *Back at midnight.* The phone stops. You go back to Emerson's room and dig half of a bagel out of your bag. You shake some instant coffee into a cup and go back to the kitchen to put water on to boil. You wonder if you can trust the water.

The phone rings.

I need to figure this out.

It rings.

Someone on the outside.

You pick it up.

"Hello?" you say brightly.

"Hi, is Graham there?"

Will, Walden, Walter, Walt.

"Hi, Walt," you reply, trying to sound older. "How are you?"

"Anna?" he falters. "Is that you?"

You laugh. "I know, it's been a long time."

"Yeah, it has," he says slowly. "You and Graham, well, are you . . . back together?"

"No. Just getting some things. For Emerson."

"Ah, okay." He pauses and you know you've thrown him off. But you need him back. You need information.

"Can I help you with something?"

"Well . . ." he hesitates again. "I've been trying to get ahold of Graham for weeks now. He's missed the last three meetings and hasn't returned my calls, so I'm getting kind of worried about him."

Meetings.

We need to meet. We have options.

"Meetings?" you ask as evenly as you can. *That's where he gets his orders.*

"Yeah," he sighs. "I mean, we used to talk all the time on the phone, and I feel like we've gotten close. And as his sponsor, I have a certain obligation, you know? I just want to know he's all right."

Sponsor.

"Sure," you say quietly. This isn't about orders.

"He's not been drinking, has he?"

You shake your head, tears filling your eyes, until you remember Walt can't see you.

"I don't know."

You hang up the phone before he can reply.

You go to Emerson's room. You shove your food and journal and clothes into your backpack. Noise is filling up your mind and you know Hannah will be here soon.

43

You wipe your eyes and walk down the street, listening. They're back at it again. You think there must be a meeting soon.

Seventy-Seven's been compromised; I'm sure of it now.

You think he's protecting her?

Yes.

That's a serious accusation.

I know.

Don't repeat it. We'll know soon enough.

You have no plan as you stumble through the cool evening, but you aren't nervous. He made your decision easy. You knew he was dangerous from the beginning, but he almost had you convinced. *It's not my thing,* you scoff, remembering his bullshit. You wonder about Emerson. You know now that she's in danger, too.

You go east on Sixty-First for a while, then head north on Goldfinch. You walk for a long time. You need to expel your frustration and you need to get him out of your head. You bypass Cameron Park because you know he'll probably look for you there. You keep going to Twenty-Ninth Street—not a great part of town, but, as always, easy to blend in. You collapse onto a bench opposite an all-night drugstore. You look around. A few people are already sleeping against buildings and on benches, so you don't think it would seem out of place if you decided to spend the night here.

You open your bag and see the half of a bagel from Jessman's, but you're on your own again now and can't afford to eat until you have to. You wish you had water for your coffee. You feel like you should stay awake until tomorrow morning, until it's light out and you feel safer, but your eyes are already glazing over and your body feels heavy. You dig your fingernails into your arm to wake yourself up. You hear shouting and look down the street to see a couple fighting outside a Laundromat. You take a breath. *Maybe I'll read for a while.*

But you take out your book and remember why you stopped reading it in the first place. The numbers, the threats, the code. The streetlight is dim, anyway.

You end up eating some of the coffee powder dry, but it doesn't do much for you and you fall asleep about twenty minutes later, your head resting on your backpack.

44

The streetlight is out when you wake up, and the air is cold. You wake with an uneasy feeling, and you know not much time has passed. You lift your head and then jolt upright. Someone's on the bench with you. She's looking at you, like she's been waiting for you to wake up.

"Hi," she smiles. "Sorry if I startled you. I'm Erica." She looks about eighteen, with long brown hair and red lipstick.

"Did Hannah send you?" you ask, edging away and clutching your bag.

She shakes her head.

"So what do you want?"

She laughs. "I thought you might be hungry. I brought you this." She holds out a burger wrapped in foil from the place down the street. You don't move.

"Why?"

She shrugs. "I know what it's like. I used to sleep out here, too."

"What time is it?"

"Eleven-fifteen."

"Okay." You rub your eyes, wishing the streetlight would come back on.

"You want this?" she asks, holding out the burger again.

You nod and take it, unwrapping it slowly. "You don't work for Casey Ephrem?"

"Never heard of her."

You shrug and take a bite and don't bother to correct her. She's watching you and you're not sure why she's still here, but there's nobody talking in your head so you think maybe she's not a Number.

"Did you run away, then?" Erica asks gently, after you finish.

"Why?"

"Just looks like you could use some help. Maybe some money."

"I guess," you reply warily.

She glances across the street, toward Kingston Avenue. A couple of girls are laughing as a cab with three or four guys drives away from them.

"You want to make fifty bucks?" she asks, turning back to you.

"Right now?"

She nods.

"How?"

"In about ten minutes a guy's going to pull up in front of that liquor store." She points across the street. "Not bad-looking," she says brightly. "And he likes redheads."

"To do what?"

"Whatever he wants."

You frown. "But what does he want from me?"

"Tonight? Just a blowjob. Right in the front seat; it'll take five minutes."

Your head starts to spin and you close your eyes. You think back to Britt and all the boys she went out with and how last year she told you Brandon Warren wanted her to give him a blowjob and when she finally did she said it wasn't so bad and she shouldn't have put him off so long. "You just have to think about something else," she said, "then it's not so bad."

"You know how to do it, right?" Erica asks.

Fifty bucks.

"Yeah," you finally say. "Sure."

You walk across the street with her and she tries to fix your hair for you, but there are so many tangles she can't brush through it and ends up just pulling it into a high ponytail.

"Your skin is great," she remarks, studying your face.

You try to breathe regularly but you're getting scared and when a red Civic pulls over to the curb you're sure you'll throw up before you can get the money.

"You're up," Erica says, but you look back at her uncertainly. "He's nice," she smiles, waving you toward the car. "His name's Joe."

You walk over and reluctantly open the car door. You look inside and see a man, dressed nicely in jeans and an Oxford shirt, smiling at you. But he's older than you expected. Maybe late-thirties. Old enough to be your father.

"Hi," he says cheerily. "Come on in."

You slide into the passenger seat. The radio's on softly, playing some kind of electronic club music, and the smell of cologne is overpowering. *Fifty bucks.*

"You're new," he says. "What's your name?"

But you can't speak. You not sure you could even move if you had to. You just look around his car, taking in the details and putting a picture of him together.

"That's okay," he laughs. "We don't have to talk." He puts his hand on your knee. "Your hair is beautiful," he says, but you're starting to hate it. You're starting to hate him—the man with the car and cologne and music and nice clothes. The man who could do this and find it so easy.

"I have to go," you whisper. But he brings out the fifty bucks and puts it on the console between you.

"You sure?" he says, moving his hand up your leg. "I'm really not so bad."

But you can't listen to him anymore, so you throw open the door and climb out and start running down the sidewalk. You pass Erica and she tries to say something to you, but you keep going. She can do it herself.

45

You play your old game, darting through alleys and double-backing along side streets until you're sure nobody's following you.

He's ordering another round.

Why?

. . .

But that wasn't our fault!

Doesn't matter.

You got this from Ninety-Nine?

Eighty-three. But it's true.

The people on the street are watching you again. They're tapping their watches and sending reports on you. Something's got them nervous and so they're closing in. You wish Hannah would come back and tell you what to do.

You didn't realize where you were running and now you're farther west than you want to be, between Jackson and Rushmore. You don't know who's watching now and you need to get out of sight, so you stop in a convenience store. You've still got food in your bag, but your throat is dry and sore so you pick out a bottle of blue Gatorade. You're shaking and you're dizzy and you forget to think, so it catches you by surprise when the clerk calls after you.

"Hey!"

You're almost out the door but you turn around.

"Are you gonna pay for that?" he demands, pointing at the bottle in your hand.

You hadn't even tried to conceal it. You picked up the bottle and were walking out the door with it because you were still thinking about Britt and the cologne and the hand on your knee and the fifty bucks and you didn't remember what you were trying to do.

He did it.

?

The elimination. There'll be another meeting soon. Tonight.
How many?
Not sure yet. A lot, though.

"I—" you begin, but you have no words. You have nothing left. You lower your eyes and stare at your hands, trying to think of something to say when another voice calls out behind you.

"It's all right; I've got it."

You turn around and see somebody coming up the first aisle to the register. An Indian guy. He holds out his hand with a smile and you give him the bottle. He's paying for your drink and telling the clerk it was just a mistake. He motions for you to walk back out with him and he hands it to you.

"Thanks," you mutter.

"You okay?" he asks, meeting your eyes.

You try to form words. You don't know who he is but you need to convince him everything's fine in case he's one of them.

"Yeah."

You look down and see he isn't wearing a watch. His eyes aren't sharp and quick like the eyes of the people on the street. You're shaking and you can still smell Joe's cologne on you but your mind is quiet for the moment.

"Are you in trouble or something?" he asks.

You peer at him. You don't know. It's past midnight and you don't feel safe outside anymore so you just want to find a place to stay for the night. *What does he know?* You feel in your pocket—you still have your knife. You just need a straight answer from somebody.

"Are you a Number?" you ask him.

"A number?"

"Yeah."

"Well, I'm twenty-three."

"Is that your number?"

"It's my age."

"No, I mean, like a code. Do they call you by a number?"

"No," he shakes his head. "No number. They call me Dev."

"Who's 'they'?"

"Everybody."

"So you're not going to a meeting tonight?"

He laughs. "A meeting? No, I don't go to meetings. I don't go to much of anything."

You hear the whispers start to rise in your head and you look down Twenty-Ninth. You see them watching you. They quickly turn away, tap their watches and try to look normal again, but you know something's happening. You wish you still had your old warehouse. But it's not safe. *Compromised.*

You turn back to Dev. You forgot he was there.

"Are you okay?" he asks again. You wonder why he's still talking to you.

"I need a place to stay," you mutter, trying to shut out the conversations that are now bombarding you. "Do you know of any empty buildings around here? Just not the warehouse on Matthias."

He pauses. "You serious?"

"Yeah."

"Did you run away or something? Where are your parents?"

"Listen, if you're not going to help me, I can find someplace on my own."

You turn away from him and start heading west. There should be some options on Masarasky.

"Hold on," he calls, jogging after you. "I know a place."

You narrow your eyes.

Fifty-Two, where've you been? There's a change of plans. He's sending in a plant.

Who?

Don't know yet. Might be a replacement.

For one of the lowers?

Yeah; we lost a lot of them.

Well, they're idiots.

"So, does it?"

"What?"

Dev is looking at you expectantly. The stars are shining off the street. The light hurts your eyes.

"The place. Does it sound okay?"

"I didn't hear you."

"Yeah, it looked like you spaced out there."

"Where is it?"

"Fifty-Third and Goldfinch."

You sigh. *Between Graham's and Yevgeny's.*

"And it's empty?" you ask doubtfully.

"Well, my friends and I live there."

You rub your eyes. This is getting too complicated.

"You want me to live with you?"

He shrugs. "It's up to you. People come in and out all the time. Some stay a few days, others a few months. There's room if you're interested."

"I can't pay you." You pause. "With anything."

"Nobody can," he laughs. "None of us have money. We're squatters, I guess."

You look back in the direction of Graham's place and wonder
a man weighed down by
if he's home yet. If Walt will call him back. When he'll put it together
down by a fifth of gin
that you're not coming back.

46

You walk back with Dev to his place. It's a vacant shoe factory, bigger than your old warehouse, with giant frosted glass windows and sawdust on the floors. Five others are there, too, smoking and listening to a radio and reading faded magazines. None of them have watches.

"Hey, guys," Dev calls out happily as they enter. "Oh," he says to you, lowering his voice, "I'm sorry, I didn't even ask you your name."

"Laika."

Why the hell not? You've got nothing to lose. Lose. It's all a game.

"Cool."

He introduces you to his friends: Alex, Josie, Michael, Rupa, and Hunter. All pretty young, friendly, easy-going. All broke and homeless. And like you, none of them have a plan.

Alex, Josie, Michael, Rupa, Hunter.

Alex, Josie, Michael, Rupa, Hunter.

Then Hannah crashes in.

You found other morons to hang out with? Congratulations.

"Hey," Josie says gently, "come sit." She gestures to a spot on the blanket. "You need to relax."

"Why?"

"It just looks like there's a lot on your mind."

You sit hesitantly and she offers you a cigarette. You give her a look.

"No funny stuff, just weed," she assures you.

"Ah," you laugh, shaking your head.

She laughs, too, and continues smoking it herself.

You look around the circle. Dev is showing Hunter a new book he found on Forty-Seventh Street, while Alex, Michael, and Rupa have started playing poker for decrepit shoe accessories they must have found around the factory. They've got oldies on the radio. They seem content. You feel a flash of anger, or maybe just envy. You wish you didn't know everything—that you would just lose the ability to hear the Numbers and their plans. Even if your dad catches you, you would have been more at peace without Hannah, without the people on the street, without your information on Graham. *Right?* Maybe that doesn't make any sense.

He's in place.

Already? Okay, who is he?

The new Sixteen. Very new.

Damn, that's a risk.

One Hundred knows what he's doing.

That's a job for a higher, though. It's too important.

It's got to seem natural, though. Sixteen's natural.

You met him?

I recruited him.

"How long have you been here?" you ask, turning to Dev. The starlight is cutting through the frosted glass now, making patterns on the floor. You don't know how it can be so bright.

"Oh, geez," he sighs, running a hand through his hair. "Over a year, I guess."

He's going to turn you in. Do you fucking realize that? Hannah's voice screeches in your head. *He might seem nice, but it's an act. He has a number. They all do.*

You bury your head in your hands and mutter, "No. No, no."

"Hey." Josie softly puts her hand on your shoulder. "What's going on?"

"I don't know," you mumble. "I don't know."

She glances at Dev.

"Is someone going to be looking for you?" he asks.

"No."

He nods but you don't think he believes you.

Any word on Seventy-Seven?

No . . . but there's more talk.

Compromised?

Right.

He'd have to be out of his mind.

"If it's okay," you say, turning to Josie, "I think I changed my mind."

"The cigarette?"

"Yeah."

"Sure."

She hands it to you. You doubt anything can make all this go away, but you have to try something.

47

You look up and there's Hannah, standing over the cot they gave you. It belonged to somebody named Germaine, but he moved on. You sit up. You don't remember falling asleep, but you look around and see everyone else is asleep, too. It takes you a minute to recall your surroundings. You see the broken, rusty sewing machines in the corner, exposed ductwork along the ceiling, sawdust that makes its way into everything and sometimes creates a haze in the air. You turn back to Hannah. She's wearing a dress, which is unusual for her. She usually visits in pajamas.

"You're dressed up," you say blankly.

"I had other plans."

She sits next to you. A clock ticks loudly, reminding you of what's happening, but you look around and there's nothing on the walls. You hold your watch next to your ear, but it's been silent since that time in the warehouse. And you need it out here.

Hannah doesn't say anything. You're sure she knows everything already.

"Is Graham Seventy-Seven?" you ask.

She pauses. "Yes."

"They think he's been compromised."

"Some of them do, yes."

You frown. "So they think he's working against them? Like double-crossing?"

She nods. "Helping you. Lying to Casey."

"Is he?"

"No."

"He's got that note on the fridge," you say slowly. "You know, the one that says '90–90.' It means he's trying to move up or something, right?"

She shrugs. "Probably." She looks around. "You're staying here?"

"Yeah," you say firmly. "I can't go back with him."

She shrugs. "It won't be any easier."

"He's a drunk."

"He's a lot worse than that."

"I'll figure it out. Don't worry."

Hannah's eyes flash. "You won't make it. They're meeting soon. Something will be decided."

"Then I'm not going to make it wherever I am."

"Fair enough."

She thinks you're being stupid again. You lie back down.

"Will you still visit me?"

"Will you still ignore everything I tell you?"

You laugh but she isn't smiling. You wave and say good night she walks out the door without making a sound.

Chapter 48

Graham

Let It Begin with Me

"You need to call the police," Anna said. "This is serious."

"I can't. You know I can't."

Graham was pacing the kitchen as he held the phone, sweating and smoking a cigarette he'd lit by holding it against a light bulb.

"But it's not just about what's best anymore. It's about keeping her alive."

"I'm going out to find her," he responded, his voice flat.

"Where?"

"Anywhere."

"She has a journal, right?"

"She took it with her."

"Why don't you come over here?" Anna offered calmly, and Graham knew she was treating him like a patient now. "It's after midnight. She could be anywhere by now."

"No," he said sharply. "She won't go far. And she doesn't have any money." He took another drag of his cigarette and pulled off his loosened tie. "I'm going to look for her."

Anna sighed but didn't say anything.

"I'll call you tomorrow," he assured her.

"I want to talk about the police then, if you don't find her. Just be careful, okay?"

"Sure."

Graham hung up the phone and tossed his tie on the table. He glanced up at the wall to check the time, but the clock wasn't there. He frowned, looking around. He moved out into the living room and saw the clock next to the door was missing, too. He went to Emerson's room. He knelt down by the bed and looked under, then pulled out Laika's messy pile of blankets. He unwrapped them carefully, revealing all four clocks from the apartment.

A knot grew hard in his throat as he covered them back up and shoved them under the bed.

He didn't like being out so late. A city's seedy underbelly is much more attractive when you're too wasted to care what happens to you.

He walked north on Prospect toward Cameron Park. He'd seen people sleep on the benches there a few times. He passed Fifty-Third and heard a siren. It still sounded distant, but a group of teenagers looked around nervously. One of them collected whatever the others were smoking and ran it over to the trash can in front of Leo's Gold and Silver. Graham walked up to the group.

"Hey," he said, trying to sound friendly. "I'm looking for someone. Maybe you've seen her?"

"Who?" one of the girls asked warily. She reached for the hand of the boy sitting next to her, their fingers entwining.

"My daughter. She's fourteen. Long red hair, black backpack. Her name's Laika."

Their faces dropped, like he'd bummed them out.

"Sorry," one of them said. "Haven't seen her."

Graham nodded, "Thanks," and kept moving.

The park was empty so he continued on toward Yevgeny's. He'd been at the restaurant until midnight, but still needed to check. The wind picked up and blew his hair forward as he turned onto Lowry. The place was deserted, as he expected. He'd check her old place, though, on Matthias.

He asked a few people on the way if they'd seen her. Nobody had, and most were too drunk or high to process the question. *That was me*, he thought with disgust. He turned on Matthias, and saw someone sitting outside the warehouse, drinking and smoking. A young guy, apparently homeless, with a large pack and a beard dotted with vomit. Graham questioned him about Laika and he waved carelessly.

"She'll turn up," he slurred. "They always miss their daddies."

"Yeah," Graham muttered, rubbing his forehead. "Have you been inside?" he asked, indicating the warehouse.

The guy shook his head. "I'll head over to Brighton Hills for the night. Better to stay in a group."

"There's a group over there?"

"Most nights, yeah."

Graham held back the fabric and peered through the window, but everything was dark.

"I'm going to check it out," he said to the guy.

"Good luck."

He lowered himself down to the milk crate and jumped to the floor. He felt around until his fingers brushed a cord. He pulled it and turned on the light.

Empty.

"Laika?" he called halfheartedly.

He looked around a little, but didn't want to stay long. He couldn't imagine what it must have been like for her, living there all that time. He was a grown man and the place gave him the creeps.

"She pretty?" the guy asked as Graham emerged from the warehouse.

"What?"

"Your daughter. Is she a good-looking girl?"

"She's fourteen," he said slowly, his voice hard.

The guy shrugged and Graham turned away because he was starting to feel his hands clench into fists. He needed to leave.

He dragged himself to Anna's place a little before seven, worn down by each depressing encounter he'd endured and each empty lead he'd followed.

Emerson was up, but she was having breakfast at the table and reading her chapter book, so she didn't look up when Graham came in.

"Hey, Em," he said with a smile. She looked up briefly.

"Hey." She turned back to her book. "Your voice sounds different."

"Yeah?"

"Scratchy."

She didn't say anything else and Anna tapped him on the shoulder, then indicated they should go back to her room to talk.

"I'll be back in a minute," he said to Emerson.

He followed Anna down the hall but stopped in the doorway to her room. He hadn't been in her bedroom yet—the one in this apartment, the one he might as well have thought of as her and Barry's room—and it was strange for him to suddenly become a part of it. But he didn't want her to see his awkwardness, so he forced himself to ignore the picture of them on her nightstand and the condom wrapper in the trash can, and walked through the door.

"So, nothing?" she asked in a low voice, turning toward Graham.

He shook his head.

"Can we call the police now?"

"Not yet."

"Graham, we are wasting time. It's not fair to her."

"If we call them, that's it. I'll never be able to help her. I'll probably never see her again." He put a hand to his temple as if that could have calmed his racing mind. "If we call them," he said, "she's back with Casey. And if he beats the shit out of her on a good day, I can't imagine what he'll do to her for running away."

Anna looked down.

"If she goes into the system," Graham continued, "no one will take the time to understand what's going on. She'll bounce from place to place and probably end up in jail. I mean, you said it was schizophrenia, right?"

"I said my gut reaction was schizophrenia, but I only spent a couple of hours with her. And I'm not a specialist."

"But your friend is—what's her name?"

"Hadar."

"Yeah," he said optimistically. "Did she agree to see her?"

"She did," Anna replied slowly. "She said it's no problem—pro bono."

"And no paperwork?"

"Right. But Graham," she murmured, "none of that matters if we can't find her."

Graham blinked. He thought back to the glimmers of hope he'd seen in Laika over the past few weeks. The time she made him dinner after his long shift. The time she went on a walk with him. The time she smiled when he told her one of Emerson's jokes. The time she told him her name.

Graham forgot where he was, and sank onto the bed and began to cry. He was used to feeling helpless, weak, out of control, dangerous, but he didn't think he'd ever felt this lost before. Anna quietly put her arm around him for a minute, maybe two, before she spoke again.

"How have your meetings been going?"

Graham looked up and wiped his eyes. He had to consider it for a moment; it had been so long since he'd thought about them.

"I stopped going."

"When?"

"A few weeks ago."

She looked away and he wished he were still out searching for Laika.

"Why?"

"It just wasn't working for me anymore," he answered, feeling himself get defensive. "And it's gotten so touchy. It's like, everybody hugs now and asks each other all these personal questions . . . you're really not supposed to do that."

"Have you talked to Walt about this?"

"No. I've been avoiding him."

"I think you should reconsider."

"Going back to AA?"

"Yes."

"Listen, I don't want to talk about this now," he murmured, feeling another wave of emotion rising in his throat. "I just want to get her back."

"We will," she said, looking at him directly. "We'll put Emerson on the bus, then we'll make a plan."

49

"Dev! Dev, wake up."

You open your eyes and see Rupa pulling at Dev's sleeve. You sit up slowly, remembering where you are. You blink a few times.

"Dev, wake up! You're late."

"What?" he groans.

"Your interview. It's already nine-thirty."

You check your watch. 9:32.

"Fuck," he mutters, sitting up and rubbing his eyes. He looks around, like he's working something out, and then collapses back onto his cot.

"Are you crazy? Get up!" she continues shrilly.

"Calm down," he murmurs, without moving. "It's too late. And it wasn't going to happen."

"What are you talking about?"

"Look," he sighs, "they were only interested because I wrote that review, right?"

"Yeah."

"So, I go in there to interview, looking like this, and I can't give them a telephone number or an address. I don't even have a photo ID. And nobody around here wants to hire a guy named Devadarshan. I don't have to tell you that."

"But they were interested. That's the point."

"Let's just forget it, all right? Doesn't matter now."

He closes his eyes like he's trying to end the conversation but Rupa leans in one more time.

"If your parents knew what you were doing here, they'd fucking kill themselves."

Dev doesn't open his eyes, so Rupa storms out, slamming the heavy door behind her. The others don't even wake up.

We just need more time, okay? Just a little.
No. Un-fucking-acceptable. Do you know what he's talking about?
Hardly ever.
He's talking about eliminating the lower thirty, smartass.

. . .

Yeah. You guys apparently aren't worth shit out in the field.
That's what he said? It's about information retrieval?
That's what everything's about.
You need coffee. Boiling water. *How do they boil water?*
Alex, Josie, Michael, Rupa, Hunter.
Alex, Josie, Michael, Rupa, Hunter.
You stumble over to Dev, feeling dizzy. He opens his eyes.
"You all right?"
You hold out your instant coffee, unsure of how to say it.
"You need some water?"
You nod.
"Yeah, we don't have that," he says, closing his eyes again. "Your best bet is the Starbucks. They might heat it up for you."
"Thanks."
You were hoping you wouldn't have to leave. But you will for this.

You're still carrying the coffee as you walk out onto the street. Watches everywhere. The people are checking and tapping them constantly, glancing at you and moving on. They all match, too: chunky and black with Velcro wristbands, like the kind you'd wear camping. Or on maneuvers. They're not just on the people now, though. Those watches start to appear on street signs, in the corners of windows, and etched into sewer grates. It's their symbol, and he's making sure you see it. He wants you to know he's winning.

50

It's not until someone nearby yells out to his friend that you realize you've been standing in the middle of the sidewalk for a long time. You check your own watch. Twenty-seven minutes. The water. You start heading east on Fifty-Third toward Ballard-Davis Road. You've seen the Starbucks on the corner but you've never been inside. When you arrive there are a lot of people outside, just standing around in groups. They always have to look. You avoid their eyes and take a few steps backward, thinking you might try somewhere else.

"Laika!"

You feel pretty numb, so it doesn't really register that someone said your name. Maybe it's not even your name. Maybe it's just another code, another Devushka. Another number. But someone's grabbing you now; you can feel arms around you, crushing you. You shriek and push at them.

"Laika, can you hear me?"

You stop. Graham's watch looks a little nicer than the ones you usually see, a little bigger, and you can hear it tick. The digitals all tick, somehow. He taps it and it stops. You look up at him.

"Was that a signal?"

"What?"

"I see them doing it, too. They tap their watches and send information. Did you tell him you found me?"

"Who?"

"I don't know what you call him," you laugh. "One Hundred or Casey?"

"No," he begins slowly. "No, I'm not . . . I mean, I don't even wear a w—"

"Never mind," you break in. "I don't want to give you more to go on."

You look at him more closely and realize he looks awful. He hasn't shaved and looks like he hasn't slept.

"I'm so glad I found you," he says shakily. You think he's going to cry, but then he starts yelling. You don't understand him for a minute. You can't tell what he's saying and he's yelling at you louder and you wince and cover your ears until he stops.

"What are you hearing?" he asks, frowning.

You shake your head.

"Will you come home now?"

"No."

"Were you looking for water?" he asks, pointing to your coffee.

You shake your head again. "I was just leaving."

"I'll get it for you." He walks toward the Starbucks. "Just give me a sec."

You could run. But you get the idea it wouldn't matter. Whatever the plan is, it doesn't look like you can stop it. And you're relieved to get your water without having to go inside.

You walk over to a bench and sit. You realize you're wearing a t-shirt and everyone you see is wearing jackets and sweaters. You can't even feel the air around you, like it has no temperature at all.

He did it. It's done.

How?

M-16.

Man.

I know.

So the new guy . . .

He's the only one left in the lower thirty right now.

Where does that leave us?

One Hundred made it pretty clear everyone under fifty is still in danger.

We need to bring him something good, then.

You shiver. You can feel the tension between the Numbers. They're getting desperate.

Graham is sitting

the last three meetings

next to you, holding out a cup of steaming water. It takes you a minute to come back.

"Thanks," you tell him, taking the cup. You pour some of the powder in and Graham hands you a coffee stirrer. He wipes his eyes. You lean back and take a few drinks. He doesn't speak until you're nearly done.

"Why'd you run off last night?"

You blink. *Was it only last night?*

"Did Walt call you back?"

"Walt?"

"Yeah. Did he call you back?"

"Wait, you talked to Walt?"

You nod. "You can't just skip those meetings, you know. You won't get better."

He just sits there for a few moments, looking like he's going to throw up.

"He said he was worried about you," you continue. "Did he call you back?"

Graham shakes his head. He rubs his face.

"I'm sorry that's how you heard. I wasn't going to meetings because I feel like I'm past that point," he says quietly. "I didn't know Walt was trying to get in touch. I was going to tell him when I was sure." His eyes are glassy, like he can't focus. "I can't get messages on that machine . . ." he trails off, looking back toward his apartment.

His talking makes you tired. You don't want to listen to his script, handed down from another higher, detailing exactly what to say and how distraught to seem and when to make his voice waver and where to put his hands. He's talking, but you're studying him. His jacket, gray and tattered, is just like one your dad used to have. You saw him in it on Thirty-Ninth. His watch is glowing and pulsing in regular intervals, alerting him to some development. But he's ignoring it, committed to his act for the moment. His face is sullen and his eyes look pained. Then you see something.

You frown and blink several times, making sure it's really there. It is. On the side of his neck he has a small tattoo, done in blue ink. It's a number.

Seventy-seven.

"I was never violent," he's saying. "I know that's what you're thinking. I know that's how it was with Casey. But that isn't me."

Seventy-Seven.

"I quit drinking nine years ago. Emerson wasn't even born yet. I did have one relapse, though . . ." he trails off, looking away. "About four years ago. I was doing really well at this other restaurant, but I was having some other problems, about the accident. Anyway, I lost my job and had to take some time off. Then I had to start over."

"When did you become a Number?"

". . . A 'Number'?"

"Did you start as a lower, or have you always been Seventy-Seven?"

"Laika," he frowns, "I don't know what that means. What are the Numbers?"

Sixteen, Forty-Five, Twenty-Three, Eighty-Two, One Hundred, Seventy-Seven, Seventy-Seven, Seventy-Seven, Seventy-Seven

"You really don't know?"

"I promise you, I don't."

"Then what's that on your neck?"

"What?" he asks, feeling around, acting confused.

"The tattoo."

His face changes. He looks scared and you know you're getting to him, cutting through his bullshit.

"There's no tattoo, Laika," he murmurs. "I swear I've never—"

"Come on!" you shout, annoyed that he thinks he can still pretend with you. "I know you're Seventy-Seven! I know you're a higher in my dad's network, okay? Just stop lying. You probably helped him eliminate the lower thirty."

Remember me? Your dad's friend.

You're shaking and you know they'll come for you now. *Where the hell is Hannah?* You've said way too much. But Graham is surprisingly calm.

"Can you tell me about the lower thirty?"

"Why?" you laugh sardonically. "They're your guys. Or they were until One Hundred killed them."

"And One Hundred is Casey?"

"Why are you pretending? Is it some kind of code and the other Numbers are going to swarm me? Is it finally over?"

He's quiet for another minute or so.

"Where did you stay last night?" he finally asks.

"Around."

"Alone?"

"No."

He sighs and looks at you sadly. "You're going to get hurt."

"Is that a threat?"

Bring him something good

"No. It means you're a kid on the street and someone will try to take advantage of you."

"Is that what you were doing?"

"No."

"No, you were just following orders," you say coldly. "Information retrieval, right?"

"Laika, I need you to listen," he pleads. "I'm not a Number. I don't wear a watch and I've never gotten a tattoo. Something is happening to you, okay? It's part of an illness. These things you're talking about . . . they're not real. Please come home so we can figure this out."

You thought he'd come up with something better. Gas-lighting you, telling you the things right in front of you aren't real is a lazy way out.

Did you hear the shots? Sixty-Eight! Are you there?

I heard. I heard three shots.

But he didn't call a meeting.

Fifty-One just told me he heard at least six.
Did you turn in your reports?
Yes.
Everyone?
Yes.
Good. We need to figure out what's going on.
This is Eighty-Three. I've got the final count.
?
Ten.
Who were they?
Take a guess.
. . . Up to forty.
Bingo.

Graham's watch is going crazy, but he doesn't look. He's watching you. The Network's ranks are being decimated and the key to his survival is sitting right in front of him.

The water.

You look down. Your cup is empty.

Goddamn it.

You did it again. Stupid again. You let him in and he got you. He slipped something into your water and you've got to leave before he gets what he came for. You stand up.

"I've got to go."

"No," Graham says firmly, rising to his feet as well. "Please, I want you to come with me. Anna and I, we have a plan—"

You run.

"Laika!"

You don't look back.

You cut through buildings and cross streets haphazardly and never look back. The Numbers are shouting. You know the remaining ten lowers are in danger. The highers are worried, too. They've got nothing to lose now. You need to hide.

Alex, Josie, Michael, Rupa, Hunter
Alex, Josie, Michael, Rupa, Hunter
Devadarshan

You think they're okay but

Alex, Josie, Michael, Rupa, Hunter
Alex, Josie, Michael, Rupa, Hunter
Devadarshan

you really don't know anything anymore.

51

When you get back to the factory everyone's gone. Dev says they try not to steal. They look for odd jobs on the street and around the city, and sometimes they beg. You lie down on your cot and try to see the ceiling through the dense fog above you. *Maybe it's smoke,* you think lazily. *Maybe we're on fire.* You close your eyes.

"Go ahead and tell me," you say. "Tell me I just fucked myself over. That Graham gets promoted and I get killed."

"I wasn't going to say that."

You open your eyes and Hannah's sitting on a wooden box next to you. She's back in pajamas, purple with silver stars. There's a ribbon in her hair. She pulls out her cigarettes.

"Then what were you going to say?"

"I think you need a new strategy."

"So you don't think it's over?"

She shakes her head, striking a match. The cigarette's in her mouth and she shields it with her hand as she lights it. "Not at all."

"So what do I do?"

"What do you think?"

"Jesus, I don't know," you sigh. "All the lowers are being eliminated. If he's killing his own people, what do you think he'll do to me?"

"It won't be pretty," she agrees.

"I can't stop my thoughts," you continue. "Graham keeps getting into my head. How can I keep them from listening? There's no way I can stop them."

You're getting upset so Hannah pulls out another cigarette for you and lights it.

"I don't smoke."

"I've heard differently," she replies with a smile. "It's weed this time. Same as Josie's."

You take it.

Hannah's wrong: there is no way out of this.

"There is a way out," she says.

"So tell me."

She shakes her head. "I'm tired of giving you all the answers. You need to think about this one yourself."

"I thought I was too stupid for that."

"Maybe," she shrugs. "Maybe not." She gets up and looks around. "You *can* stop your thoughts, though. You can make everything stop, if you want to. They don't have to win this."

You know she's not going to tell you what she's talking about so you don't say anything. You suddenly wish Dev and the others would come back. "I'm going to sleep for a while."

"Sure."

Hannah leaves another cigarette for you on the box before she walks to the door.

"Do you still have your knife?" she asks, turning around.

"Yeah."

"Good. Stay safe."

She leaves and you drift into an uneasy sleep.

52

Dev was born in Pondicherry, on the coast of southern India. The only child in a rich family, his parents were obsessed with his success in school. He wasn't interested in much besides getting high with his friends, but he played along, knowing it was his ticket out. He aced his exams and, at twenty, they sent him to the States to study chemical engineering. But it was harder than he thought. He tried to keep up with his studies and his drugs, but he couldn't do both. He hated it, and he couldn't tell his parents. He eventually failed out, and couldn't tell them that, either.

You learn all this at night, after the others have gone to bed and you've slept all day so you aren't tired yet. Dev brings out some kind of cigarette he calls "block"; he says it's better than pot and he really needs to relax tonight. You've just learned that the rest of the lowers, except for the new Sixteen, have been eliminated, so you accept when he offers you one.

"I'm just trying to keep my head above water," he smiles. He cups his hands around the cigarette as he lights it.

"You can't go back home?"

"No," he shakes his head. "I won't do that again. I was never happy." He takes a long draw on the cigarette, then exhales deeply. "I mean, I always felt claustrophobic in India—like it was suffocating me. Here, I don't have shit," he laughs, "but at least I can breathe again."

You nod.

"So, what about you?" he asks with a smile. "What are you running from?"

I should just kill you now, Laika. I don't give a shit what these Numbers think they know. They think the Network is everything, but it's all a game. And I'm just about bored of it.

"Laika?"

". . . Yeah."

"Sorry, I probably shouldn't have asked you that."

"What?"

"What you're running from."

"Oh . . . I didn't hear you." You blink hard and look back up at Dev. "A group home."

"Like a foster care kind of thing?"

"Yeah."

"Geez, I'm sorry. That's really shitty."

There is a way out.

"Thanks."

"Well, I'm glad you ran into me."

You don't really know how it happens but you go to bed with him. There's an office in the back of the building and he asks you to go with him, and for once you're the only one inside your head and it feels like he's really talking to you. And you go. It's your first time. It's not horrible and it's not great, but you like being with him.

It's six in the morning and everyone is still asleep. Dev brings you back water for your coffee.

"They triple filter it," he says. And then he smiles, and for the first time you wonder if maybe he's the new Sixteen.

53

"Do you want to come out with us today?"

Michael's sitting at a table, finishing a drawing he's been working on for a few days. It's of a shack overgrown with moss that he once saw on a mountain pass. For some reason it stuck in his mind.

You shake your head. "I'm okay."

Josie looks up from her book.

"When's the last time you went outside?"

"I don't know."

"Don't you need food?"

"I still have some," you say, indicating your bag.

"We can always get you something, too." She smiles then returns to her book.

"Absolutely," Michael adds distractedly.

You like them best of the group, aside from Dev. They're younger, both nineteen, and have a friendly, bohemian way about them. They want to help you. You're confident they aren't Numbers. But Dev . . . something about him leaves you unsettled. He's too charming, too kind. Too natural.

When you first met him and asked him about the Numbers, the meetings, when you spaced out as he talked, he wasn't bothered. He didn't seem surprised. As if he knew it was coming.

The plan. The report.

He's nine years older than you are. He's smart. *He wants something.*

"What do you guys think of Dev?" you ask suddenly, looking up at Josie and Michael.

"Dev?" Josie frowns. "What do you mean?"

"You've known him awhile, right?"

"Right."

"Is he, you know, a good guy?"

"Sure. He's a lot of fun," Josie says. "I really think he cares about us, too."
Michael snorts faintly.

"What?" you ask, turning to him. "You don't like him?"

"He's all right," Michael smiles. "But I think a lot of it's an act."

I recruited him.

"How do you mean?" you ask slowly.

"I've just seen him out, you know, when it's just the two of us. Frankly, he can be kind of an asshole. I think he puts on a good face on when the group's together." Michael looks at you closely. "Do you like him or something?"

"I don't know. What's he done?"

"He robbed a guy once, out on the street. Scared him, too. He really thought Dev was going to kill him. I mean, he makes a big show about how we shouldn't steal and should try to find meaningful work, blah, blah, blah. Then he goes and pulls a knife on this poor guy, like it was nothing."

"He had a knife?"

"Oh, yeah."

Josie shrugs. "It's not easy, living like this. And he's been doing it longer than we have. I still think he's pretty decent."

"He harasses girls, too, you know," Michael says.

Josie laughs. "Yeah, he did say he liked my dress the other day."

"Did he try to rape you after that?"

"What are you talking about?"

"That's what he did the other night. Just a few weeks ago."

"You serious?"

"Yeah," he replies, his face stern. "It was pretty fucked up. We were out with Hunter, trying to catch the restaurants at closing before they toss all their food. We saw this group of high school girls cross the street ahead of us, and Dev said we should go around and cut them off at the next street. I asked him what he was doing but he just kept laughing and said it would be hilarious. We circled around and he told us to wait in this alley, and then he ran up and grabbed two girls hanging a bit back from the group. He shoved one at us and slammed the other against the wall and started feeling her up. I couldn't believe it. And the girls were too scared to even move. But then Hunter grabbed Dev and pulled him off and I told the girls to run. But later, he still thought the whole thing was a joke. And he was actually mad that we spoiled it."

There's a break in the case. Did you file a report?

Yeah, but it's not me. It's Sixteen.

Already?

He knows what he's doing.

He'll replace a higher soon, then. Maybe even me.
You've done good work; don't think like that.
Can I ask you something? I mean, without the murmurs.
Sure.
Do you think One Hundred . . .
?
. . . do you think he's killing us just for fun?
. . . Yes.
Then we don't have much time. We have to get to Sixteen.

"Jesus," Josie breathes. "That's terrible."

"Well, that's Dev," Michael laughs scornfully.

"I was more wondering," you begin carefully, "if you ever thought he might be working against you. Like he might turn you in."

"To the police?" Josie asks.

"Yeah. Something like that."

"He'd be dumb as shit if he did," Michael laughs. "With all the drugs he does, Dev would be the first one arrested."

You can make everything stop, if you want to.

"So maybe he'd work for someone else. Someone who'd protect him from the police." You're thinking aloud and forgot the others were in the room.

"What makes you think he's interested in turning us in?"

They're both looking at you, frowning. You need to stop talking. It's getting harder to separate your thoughts from your words. You need to stop talking.

"Nothing, really," you say. "I just realized I don't know much about him."

"I'd keep it that way," Michael says, turning back to his work.

54

You're outside. You think it's the first time in two weeks. You're out of food, but that's not what drew you out. Dev and the others always bring you something back. Hannah told you to meet her here, on this same bench, outside the Starbucks. She's never done that before—sent for you through her thoughts—so you think it must be important.

You thought it would be nice to breathe in fresh air again, but you can't stop thinking about how stupid this is. *Out in the open, I'm caught.*

"You're fine," Hannah says with slight annoyance. She comes around from behind the bench and sits next to you. "If those idiots haven't gotten to you yet, you can afford a few minutes out here with me."

"So, what did I do?"

"About what?"

"About the plan. I must have done something wrong for you to want to meet this way."

"I thought you should get out."

"Why?"

She squints up at the sky. "To see what you're missing. I mean, can you even remember what it was like before the Numbers?"

"Yeah," you begin, confused, "I was living with their boss."

"Oh, yeah," she replies vaguely. "That must have been something. Casey Ephrem."

"Have you met him?"

"I've seen him. But he hasn't seen me, I hope. I've been in a lot of those meetings."

"What did you think of him?"

"I can't imagine him ever having a family."

You nod. That sounds about right.

"So, I haven't done anything wrong?"

"I wouldn't go that far." Hannah turns to face you squarely. "We need to talk about Dev."

"I know."

"You're sleeping with him."

"I guess."

"You're letting him bring you food."

"I can't go outside."

"You are outside."

"You know what I mean."

"I'm finding that's rarely the case these days."

You shake your head. Now she's just trying to rile you.

"Do you not remember what Graham was doing?" she presses. "He was getting to your thoughts by poisoning your food. What's to stop Dev from doing the same thing? What about the drugs he gives you?"

"So you think he's a Number?"

"Yes."

"Is he Sixteen?"

She pauses. "I don't know. I haven't been able to confirm it."

"So you don't really know?"

"It's a feeling. And I know you think so, too. I can hear you, remember?"

Of course. I can never fucking forget.

"Then don't be stupid," she snaps. "You're giving him access. If he is Sixteen, then he's the best thing they have going right now."

They think the Network is everything, but it's all a game.

You lean forward on the bench and bury your face in your hands. You honestly can't remember what it was like before the Numbers. Maybe they were always there.

"Don't listen to Casey," Hannah says, her voice a little softer. "He's doing what he thinks will help him win. The Network is real."

You lift your head slowly. Murmurs. They're lit again, alerting.

"I need this to be over."

Hannah watches you for a moment.

"Do you really?"

"Yeah."

"Then you need to think. You need to make a plan. Remember, I can't answer this one for you."

Chapter 55

Graham

I'm a Friend

Graham opened the door slowly and saw Dr. Schwartz at his desk, writing. He smiled but didn't look up.

"Graham," he began, "Your session is halfway over. Why don't we just reschedule—"

Then he looked up. He stopped talking. He rose from his chair and motioned for Graham to come in.

"Are you all right?" Schwartz asked, guiding Graham to his usual chair.

Graham collapsed and shook his head. He took a few breaths and leaned back, covering his eyes with his hand.

"What happened?" Schwartz pressed, with more emotion in his voice than Graham had heard before. "Are you drinking again?"

"No." He sat up. "But I just talked to my sponsor. I'm going to go back to the meetings."

"You'd stopped going to meetings?"

"Yeah."

Schwartz reached for his notepad and Graham knew he would add it to the list of all of the other things he'd withheld.

"Are you feeling driven to drink?"

"Not really. But I'm feeling out of control, and I'm not sure where that'll go."

"What happened?"

"It's Laika."

"Things aren't working out?"

Graham took a breath and shook his head. "She ran away."

"From your place?"

"Yeah."

"Why?"

"It doesn't matter," Graham replied irritably. "She's living with this random group of people, and her illness is getting worse and she won't let me help her."

Schwartz got up and went to his desk. He pulled a bottle of water from the bottom drawer and handed it to Graham. "But you know where she's living now?"

He nodded. "I go by a few times a day, just to check on her."

"How do you know she's getting worse?"

"Because the first time I saw her, after I'd been out all night looking for her, she started telling me things I couldn't understand—things she was seeing and hearing that weren't real. It was like she was dreaming. She told me to admit I'm part of this conspiracy to send her back."

"So she ran from you again?"

"Yeah." Graham took a long drink. His head was starting to pound and he just wanted to leave. To bring her back.

"How long ago was this?"

"I don't know; a couple weeks?"

"And how have you been sleeping?"

"I sleep every third or fourth night."

Schwartz wrote something down, then looked back through a few pages of his notes. He went to his desk and pulled out a different pad.

"I'd like to prescribe you something. I think you're ready."

"No," Graham said quickly, holding up his hand to stop him. "I don't need it."

Schwartz frowned. "You're going to make yourself sick."

"I don't need the sleep."

"What do you do while you're awake?"

"I've been reading books," he said slowly. "Articles, case studies. Anything."

"Schizophrenia?"

Graham nodded.

"What are you hoping to find?"

"I don't know," Graham smiled miserably. "I guess something that tells me I'm wrong."

Schwartz walked back to his chair but brought the prescription pad with him.

"How's work?"

"About the same."

"Even with all this?"

"Jack's been giving me shorter shifts, I guess so I don't get overworked and mess up more."

"So he's cutting your hours?"

"Yeah."

"Can you afford that?"

"It's better than getting fired. And I think that's my other option."

"Okay." Schwartz looked thoughtful for a moment, then began writing on the prescription pad. "I think you need these now," he murmured, "but obviously I can't make you take them." He tore off the slip of paper and handed it to Graham. "Just keep it in case you change your mind."

Graham nodded and took the prescription, stuffing it in his shirt pocket. He didn't want to think about what Laika was doing now—about her stealing and trying to navigate this new group and hiding from her delusions. And how his biggest problem was a sleepless night that could be fixed with a single pill.

As he left Dr. Schwartz's building Graham tossed the paper into the trash can on the sidewalk. He didn't care if he ever slept again.

56

You're writing again. It helps you be more careful about Dev. You steal your own food now. You watch his behavior closely. His appearance. He doesn't have a tattoo like Graham, but maybe those are just for the highers. You still hope he's not a Number, but you have to be smart.

You detail your observations in your journal. You've also started writing down your conversations with Hannah and the exchanges you overhear from the Numbers, or whatever you can remember from them. It's hard to keep everything straight.

Dev and Hunter walk in and you look up. Hunter slams the door behind him. Rupa looks over at you and makes a face like she's annoyed they came back. You can write around her—she never asks what you're doing—but not anyone else.

Dev turns back to Hunter, as if he forgot to tell him something, but Hunter holds his hands up.

"Get away from me," he says seriously. "I told you; I'm done."

You slide your journal into your backpack.

Dev shrugs. "Fine."

"What's going on?" Rupa asks, setting her book aside.

"Not much," Hunter says, collapsing into a chair. "Dev just tried to get me arrested."

at least I can breathe again.

At twenty-eight, Hunter is the oldest of the group. He's big, grungy, and has a faint Tennessee drawl. Dev doesn't like him. He told you if Hunter wasn't so good at scoring drugs, he'd get rid of him. That's when you realized Dev was in charge of the group.

"Hunter, you're full of shit," Dev replies. "It was an honest mistake."

"So what happened?" Rupa asks, a narrowed eye trained on Dev.

"We're way west on Baltimore, right? The guy at Trainer's Hardware had some work for us last week, so we were waiting for it to open." Hunter takes a breath and glances at Dev. "We hear this guy behind us say, 'So, which one of you is dealing today?' Dev automatically, *automatically*, turns around and says, 'He is,' and points to me. The guy wasn't a cop, it turns out, but some junkie who saw us from behind and thought we were his dealers. But, man," Hunter shakes his head, "it took less than a second for him to throw me under the bus."

"It wasn't like that," Dev groans. "Don't you think if one of us was caught, the other would be, too?"

"Didn't seem like you were thinking it through back there. You were desperate, man."

"Dev, that's pretty low," Rupa sighs.

Devadarshan.

I don't have to tell you that.

Dev slams his bag to the ground. He's getting mad. He won't say anything, though. He doesn't talk when he's mad.

You need to think.

Hunter goes back outside to get some air and Rupa walks over to Dev, sits next to him in Hunter's chair.

"What is going on?" she asks him pointedly. "First you piss off Alex somehow, and now Hunter? Are you on your period?"

"Leave me alone, okay? Stop trying to be my big sister."

"I don't know what else to do."

"You could mind your own damn business."

Rupa laughs. "Okay, but nobody else understands where you're coming from. You've got to be careful, Dev, because right now you're just another arrogant, strung-out Desi trying to get back at his parents. And it's never going to work."

He doesn't say anything for a while, so Rupa stands up.

"I'm going to find Hunter," she mutters, and walks outside.

You swear you hear a clock ticking again. Just like at Graham's. You have to be careful. *If Sixteen's as good as they say, he'll have different methods. Better ways to get what he wants.*

Dev comes over and sits on your cot. Nobody's around so he kisses you.

"I'm sorry about that."

"What?"

"I must be coming off as a real asshole."

You pause. "You'd really turn him in like that?"

"It was a reaction," Dev answers, his voice strained. "It's what we do. We have to look out for ourselves, or we won't make it."

You look down. His hands are shaking. That confuses you because he's always so confident, so in control.

"I don't know," he sighs. "Maybe I shouldn't have left things like that."

He cracks his knuckles. There's a smudge of something on his thumb. He's watching the door. You blink, clearing your vision, trying to look closer.

"I don't know," he says again.

It's not a smudge. It's writing.

"Do you think I should go talk to him?"

A tattoo.

he's the best thing they have going right now.

Sixteen.

"Yes," you say calmly, looking back up at him. "You should go talk to him."

There has to be a way out.

"Okay." He smiles warmly and gives you another kiss. "I won't be long."

You watch the door for another two minutes after he leaves. You don't have much time. You walk over to his bag and carefully unzip it. Weed. Two novels. A pack of cigarettes. Beef jerky. A bagel. Three bananas. There's something at the bottom, illuminating a portion of the darkness with a blue glow. You dig down and pull it out. His watch. *Murmur.* You've never seen one this close and you don't understand it. The flashing alerts are in code—a jumble of letters and numbers to you—but you see his number stays solid at the top. Sixteen.

You put everything back and replace the bag on the floor carefully.

You need to think. You need to make a plan. Remember, I can't answer this one for you.

You need to leave.

That must be what Hannah's talking about. She's telling you everyone here is against you. You'd have to go far, maybe out of the country, but you could start again.

Over the next few days you finalize your plan. You'll steal something nice—a perfume set, maybe—and sell it on the street so you'll have enough for a bus ticket. You'll go back up north—they won't expect that—and you'll keep going into Canada. You'll burn your journal. You'll burn everything you own. You'll start over.

57

On Tuesday Dev asks you to come out with him. You brush him off, as usual, but he says you should see how he does a job—see how easy it could be for you. You watch him as he talks, glancing at his Network tattoo. You're still not sure about going out with him but he tells you it won't take long and you'll probably get ten bucks out of it, so you agree and leave the factory with him a little after noon.

It's less than two miles to Vons supermarket on Redding Avenue. There are lots of people out and it's a nicer area and you never go to places like this because you can't blend in, so you wonder what he's thinking. But then you remember he's not here to steal. That's not his thing.

But you don't really want to know what his thing is. He wears his murmur all the time now, and doesn't seem to care that you see it. It glows constantly and he only taps it a few times a day. You can tell he's different, he's never on edge or worried, so you think he must be an important part of the Network. But you have to play along, for just a little while longer. Soon you'll be gone.

You both walk up to the front doors of Vons but he says there's no need to go in. You just have to wait. He glances casually at the people leaving the store but you're not sure what he's looking for. After a few minutes he tells you to back up a little and act like you're not with him. You move a few feet away to the bench by the crosswalk and grab a renter's guide so you can pretend to read.

"Hi," Dev says brightly to an older man walking out of Vons. "Got any spare change?"

The man looks up and smiles uncomfortably. He's wearing jeans and a camouflage jacket and a navy cap that says "US Air Force" in yellow letters.

"Sorry," he says, lowering his eyes. "Not today."

The man starts to turn away, but Dev isn't finished.

"I'm sorry, but you're a veteran, right?" he asks politely. "Air Force?"

The man turns back and smiles again. "That's right. Twenty–seven years."

"Wow." Dev shakes his head. "My dad was in the Air Force. I'm in the Army Reserve." He flashes a charming smile. "Best thing I've got going."

"That's great," he replies.

"Yeah," Dev continues, "I've been thinking of joining up, you know, full time. I feel like I could use the direction."

The man nods and looks thoughtful, but doesn't say anything.

"Anyway," Dev smiles, "thanks for your service. That's really incredible."

He turns and starts walking back toward the store like he might go in, but the man stops him.

"Hey," he calls, digging in his pocket. "Wait a sec." Dev comes back over and the man hands him a bill. "Take care of yourself, huh?"

Dev nods and shakes his hand, then watches him walk through the parking lot before joining you on the bench.

"What'd I tell you?" he says happily, handing you the ten-dollar bill. "Beats the hell out of stealing, doesn't it?"

"I guess."

"You want to give it a try?"

You laugh. "No way."

"Come on," he says. "You just have to smile, then make up a story."

"I think it's harder than it looks."

He shrugs. "Maybe." He takes your hand and smiles. "But you should practice."

"You don't need to practice," you reply, glancing down at the murmur that's now touching your wrist. "You just look at people and they give you money. That's what Alex said."

He laughs. "Well, I guess I'm just a natural."

58

It's Saturday. They're all gone, out on the street looking for work and hand-outs. Dev took his bag. His watch. The Numbers are all talking about him now; they say he's bringing in more information than the highers. They're getting agitated. They say he won't tell anyone his methods. They think he's setting them up for elimination.

Elimination. It's all over.

You decide you'll leave your bag so Dev won't know you're gone right away. You'll keep the clothes you're wearing and your knife. The journal can burn. You hold your knife and turn it around in your hand thoughtfully.

you need a new strategy.

Something is gnawing at you but you can't place it. You feel like you're being stupid again.

Come on, Hannah, just tell me.

This is too important.

That's why you need to tell me.

I can't end it for you.

The knife turns sweaty in your hand. You look down at it.

Of course.

It's not an escape. That isn't good enough. It's not a fantasy of running to Canada. Why would they leave you alone there? Why would he quit just because you ran?

That's not what she's talking about.

You can make everything stop, if you want to.

Elimination.

Now.

It makes perfect sense.

They don't have to win this.

You can end it. You can win it.

You open the knife and test the sharpness of the blade on your finger. You don't even feel it.

So, what, Hannah? Did I solve your puzzle? Is this my way out?

You need it to be over, right?

Absolutely.

Then, congratulations.

Congratulations. You smile. You will shut down the Network.

"Hey, Laika."

You didn't see him come in.

"Dev."

"You okay?" He points to your finger that's now dripping blood onto the floor.

"Yeah. It's nothing." You wrap the end of your shirt around it. "You're back already?"

"I wanted to see you."

"Really?"

He smiles broadly and you understand. But he must know that you've figured him out. You're sure he reads your thoughts. He wouldn't be turning in so many reports if he wasn't. And after all this, he still expects you to sleep with him.

"I was going to read for a while," you say, pulling out one of Graham's books from your bag.

"That can wait."

He takes the book from you. He touches your hair.

We've got a new alert. Sixty, have you seen this one before?

No.

He grips your face and kisses you.

Guys, that's the Endgame Warning.

What the hell is that?

Operatives activate it if they believe the target has become a plausible threat.

Devushka? No.

You push him off. So he *does* know what you're going to do. He read your plan already.

"What's the matter?"

"Just stop, all right?"

You're not giving him anything else. It's all part of his angle. His report.

I'm glad you ran into me

You try not to think about it. You try not to imagine your dad giving him orders to sleep with you.

"You're kidding, right?"

He's angry. You don't care.

Are you listening now, asshole? I am a plausible threat.

"No. I'm going out for a while."

You make a move toward the door but he pushes you against the wall.

"Not yet."

Who set it off?

. . .

Well?

The only one of us who's going to live.

You push him back, harder. You don't have time for this.

"Fuck off, Dev. It's not happening."

Sixteen.

He hits you.

Not a punch, just a fairly inexperienced slap across the face. Then he slams you back against the wall. Pain radiates through your shoulder blades.

"I don't think that's true," he says in a low voice.

He runs his hands over your body.

Did One Hundred say that?

One Hundred?

Yeah.

I heard he's ordering another round tonight.

He holds you still with one hand against your collarbone while he unbuttons his pants.

Well, it's been nice working with you.

Likewise.

59

You blink. Dev is on the ground. Your mind is starting to clear, but you're not sure what happened. Someone's on top of him, punching him, yelling at him. You're putting it together now: the jacket, the voice, the toaster-hair.

Dev's yelling now, too, and bleeding, but Graham's not letting up. Dev eventually gets a shot in—a kick to his stomach—then staggers to his feet.

"What the fuck?" he yells, holding up his hands. "Who are you?"

"Get out."

"What?"

Dev looks at you, as if he expects backup. But you're not even listening.

Did One Hundred send him? Maybe the Numbers decided on their own. Elected Graham. They've got nothing to lose now.

"Get out."

Dev doesn't move.

"I will kill you," Graham says simply. He takes a step toward him, which seems to break Dev's trance.

"Okay, man. Fine."

Dev scowls and grabs his bag. He wipes blood from his nose. You wonder where he'll go, looking like that, and what he'll tell the others. Graham watches him leave. He seems lost in thought for a moment before he turns to you. He's breathing heavily. He's shaking.

"I told you," he laughs anxiously. "I told you, Laika. You come out on the street, you open yourself up to the scum of the earth. Guys like that," he gestures toward the door, "they're professionals. They know what they're doing."

You all know what you're doing.

"How did you know I was here?"

"I've known for a while."

"How?"

"I followed you." He wipes his forehead. "I saw you after work one day, on my way home. I wanted to make sure you were okay."

"You didn't say anything."

You didn't file a report.

"I thought you'd run again if you knew I'd found your place. So I walk by on my way to work and on my way home. You always seemed to be here; I know you don't like to go outside."

"Yeah."

You both stand in silence, breathing. He seems to be calming down. He touches his stomach.

"Oh, Jesus," he says suddenly, walking over to you. "Are you okay? I mean, are you hurt? I'm sorry, I didn't even ask."

At first, you think he's making fun of you, the insignificance of your injuries. A slightly warm patch on your cheek, a sore back. A self-inflicted finger wound. But he looks worried.

Seventy-Seven.

"I'm fine."

"Has he done that before?"

"No."

"Really?"

"You don't believe me?"

"No, I do. You just didn't seem that surprised. Like it was normal."

Normal.

"Honestly, I don't really remember."

"Okay," he nods. "It's okay."

You slide down to the floor and Graham sits as well.

Nothing to lose.

"So why didn't you file a report?" You watch him carefully.

"A report?"

"Once you knew where I lived. That would have gotten you a promotion, or at least kept you from elimination."

"With the Numbers?" he asks slowly.

You roll your eyes. He's acting again.

"Right."

"I don't know," he replies, frowning. "I really don't want to tell anyone where you live. I don't want you to get hurt."

Not until you get paid. Maybe get a spot in the nineties.

"Do you think Dev is after your number?"

"Who's Dev?"

"The guy you just beat the shit out of."

"Is Dev a Number?"

"You didn't see? It's on his thumb. Took me a while, but I found it."

"I didn't see. Remember, I was beating the shit out of him."

"Come on, Graham. I know you already know. I can hear all of you, remember? The Numbers are always talking about him. He's doing better than most of the highers."

"So, he's a . . . lower?"

He's good.

"Sixteen."

"And you hear everyone? All the time?"

"Enough to know what's going on."

"Do you ever hear me?"

"No."

"And you think Dev's trying to get a better number—my number?"

"Wouldn't you?"

"I guess."

You look over at Graham's watch. It's dark for now. But soon Dev will file another report and the lights will go crazy. Your dad will kill another level of Numbers. It won't be long before they're all eliminated. Then it's just you and him.

It's all a game.

And I'm just about bored of it.

Graham's standing up now, looking at you expectantly.

"What?" you ask him.

"We should go now," he says, "before they come back."

"What do you mean? Where?"

"Home."

I stared at it for just a second

just a second

"No way."

but it was too long.

"What, you think you can still stay here?" he exclaims. "With him?"

You shrug.

Graham rubs his face thoughtfully.

"But I thought Dev was a big threat, right? He's trying to move up, get all the information? You need to get away from him," he says firmly. "Don't let him get what he wants. Obviously I didn't do a great job. Do the Numbers talk about me?"

"Not anymore."

"You see? Maybe he's already replacing me."

"Then you'll be eliminated."

"I'll be okay."

How about a much

"Come with me," he says gently, handing you your bag. "Emerson's been asking about you. She misses you."

about a much older brother.

The Numbers are quiet.

Hannah's quiet.

You go with him.

Chapter 60

Graham

I've Been Thinking

Graham didn't say much as they walked home. He knew Laika needed time to process what was happening and he was still seething.

I would have killed him.

It scared him a little, because part of him was disappointed when Dev left. Part of him wanted to go through with it.

Graham breathed in deeply and glanced over at Laika. She walked slowly, he noticed, because she was looking at everyone they passed. Everyone was a threat to her. She wasn't paying attention to Graham, so he started watching her carefully. She'd denied it, but he was looking her over for signs Dev had hurt her before. Her throat, her face, her arms. She was still wearing short-sleeves, he noticed. There was nothing he could see—that scar had always been above her eyebrow.

Then he frowned. There was something; there was a dark bruise on her left wrist.

"What happened there?" Graham asked as softly as he could, but she still jumped a little, startled by his voice.

"What?"

"Your wrist," he said, pointing. "What happened?"

"I don't know," she said slowly, rubbing it with her other hand.

"You don't know?"

"I don't remember."

But her eyes glazed a little, like she was remembering right now.

Graham squeezed his hands a few times, a vain attempt to diffuse his building anger.

He'd known guys like Dev before. In school. In New York. In AA. Alcoholics even had a name for it: thirteenth stepping.

He saw it in action more than once, most recently from a guy he had actually liked. Garrett Mills. A friendly, talkative librarian in his late forties with a northern accent. Graham had gotten to know him a little, and was always happy to talk to him after the meetings were over. But he saw a change in Garrett as soon as Rachel arrived. Her first meeting ever, she had never shared her addiction with anyone before. She was twenty-six. Garrett shamelessly fawned over her, listened to her story with a pained expression on his face, and by the end of the night had offered to be her sponsor. After a few weeks it was clear they were seeing each other.

"What are you doing?" Graham had asked him one night, when Rachel was talking to the group leader.

"What do you mean?" he smiled.

"I mean Rachel. This is treatment for her, you know."

"Graham," he said patiently, "when's the last time you got laid by a girl in her twenties?"

"That doesn't matter. She needs this and you're ruining it."

Garrett shrugged and looked toward her. "She doesn't seem to mind."

And just as Graham had seen before, it went on for a few months, until a younger, more vulnerable member joined the group, and Garrett was gone.

He'd known people like that forever, and now one of them had gotten to his kid.

"Was it Dev?" Graham asked, trying to keep his voice casual. *How many times has he done it and made you think it was normal?*

"I don't think so."

He didn't want to push her, so he left it at that and focused on the fact that he had her back.

They both kept walking silently for a while, but when Graham saw the ice cream place on Fifty-Third—the one Emerson liked because it had coconut mocha swirl—he asked if she wanted to stop.

"That's okay," she said, glancing at the crowded shop with the line spilling out the door.

"Really? No ice cream?"

Laika shook her head. "We should get back to your place."

He nodded, still having to remind himself she wasn't like other kids. She couldn't be out in the open anymore. She was exposed and she couldn't stop studying the faces of everyone who passed by. He knew her illness exhausted her, but it seemed her life had already set her up for an unimaginably hard road. Graham watched as she whispered something to herself, a thick hair band now covering her bruised wrist. She wasn't really a kid at all anymore.

They walked into the apartment. Graham told Laika she looked tired and said she should sit down, and he'd put her bag back in Emerson's room. She gave it to him reluctantly and collapsed onto the living room couch.

He moved swiftly into Emerson's room and opened the bag. He dug around until he found her journal. He paused, waiting to hear her coming, but there was only silence. He opened up the front cover and was surprised to find exactly what he was looking for. *Ephrem.* Her name, Laika Ephrem, was scrawled across the inside cover. Graham closed the journal and shoved it back in her bag.

61

"Isn't Emerson sleeping in her room again?" you ask Graham as he comes out of her room.

You feel strange, sitting on his couch again. You don't know how long it's been since you were here, but you're pretty sure nothing's changed.

"She has been. But she won't mind moving again. Really."

"No," you say. "I'll sleep here."

"It's up to you. You want me to bring your bag back, then?"

You nod and he walks away.

You glance rapidly around the room, trying to find any evidence that he's still important to the Network. But it all looks the same. You can see part of the kitchen—Anna's number, Wile E. Coyote, the roosters, all still there. You'll look around more carefully when he's gone.

I haven't been able to confirm it.

"Hannah thinks he might have put something in the drugs," you say suddenly, remembering as he returns. "Dev, I mean. And in the food, like you did."

Graham frowns quizzically for a minute, like he didn't understand what you said.

"Drugs?" he says finally. "He gave you drugs?"

"They all smoke," you reply. "You smoke, right? It's not a big deal."

"What do they smoke?"

"Just weed. And Dev had something called block."

"That's opium."

You shrug. "That's not so bad."

"But you said he put something in it."

"Hannah said that, not me."

"Hannah's one of the girls living there?"

"No. I don't know where she lives."

"Then how did you meet her?"

"I've known her for a while," you say, unable to focus on him. "She helped me figure out that he's Sixteen. She's been in a lot of the meetings."

Graham's quiet and you realize everything's quiet. You think it's the longest that Hannah and the Numbers have let your mind rest. You wonder what that means.

"What do you mean about the food?"

"What food?"

"You said Hannah told you Dev was putting something in the food, like I did. What does that mean?"

"The poison, or whatever it was. The stuff that let you read my thoughts."

Graham looks scared again and you start to relax. He really had no idea you were onto him. He doesn't seem like higher material. You're looking at him, expecting him to deny it and keep pretending, but he's not talking. He's waiting.

"Are you going to tell me I'm wrong?" you ask.

He shakes his head.

"Then, what?"

"That's why you stopped eating here?"

"Yeah."

"How did you eat?"

"Same way I did before I met you."

"If I told you there was nothing in the food now, would you believe me?"

"No."

Graham sighs. "Okay," he says, reaching into his back pocket, "this is what we'll do, then." He takes a few bills out of his wallet. "Take this to the store and get your own food, okay? You can keep it in the kitchen, in your room—wherever you want. I won't touch it. And just tell me when you need more; I don't want you stealing."

You take the money hesitantly. You expect to hear something, to have some kind of direction from Hannah and the others, but there's nothing. Not even static. Maybe they've left you.

"Did you figure out a new way to do it, then?" you ask quietly, putting the money in your pocket. "A better way to read them—to hear the Numbers?"

"No. I don't care about the Numbers. I don't talk to any of them . . . I'm done with the Network."

"If that were true you'd be dead."

It's up to Seventy! Guys, where are you?

Seventy-Three here.

Eighty here.

Anyone else?

. . .

It's up to Seventy.

Fuck. He's speeding up.

Into the highers, now.

Nobody's safe. We've got to make a move.

You feel for your knife in your pocket.

". . . I've done it before," Graham's saying. "You don't have to worry about me."

make a move

"You're in the next group," you say, almost to yourself.

"What?"

"He just killed Fifty to Seventy."

"Did he tell you that? Did you hear him just now?"

You shake your head. "But he's speeding up again. For a while it was groups of ten."

Graham sits back for a moment. "What happens when everyone's eliminated?"

"I don't know."

"But Dev is Sixteen. How is he still alive?"

"He's a replacement," you say, rubbing your eyes. "He's young with not much training, so he got a low number, but they say he's a natural. I guess they'll just make him a higher soon. If they don't kill him."

Graham nods. He gets up and goes to the kitchen and you see him writing on a notepad. He's writing for a long time and your pulse starts to quicken and your hands start to sweat.

they say he's a natural

"What are you writing?" you call, a note of panic in your voice.

"Just needed to write myself a note. Sorry, I just remembered. I've got to do that sometimes—for the AA meetings." He stuffs the papers into his pocket and comes back into the room. "Can I ask you something?"

"What?"

"It's about Casey."

"Okay."

"Can you tell me the first time he was violent?"

"Ever?"

"That you remember."

"I don't know. Why?"

"I guess I'm just trying to figure a way out of this Network thing. And elimination. Maybe if I knew more about him—"

You narrow your eyes. "You don't want to know more about him."

"I just want a better idea of what I'm dealing with."

Maybe you've *been compromised,* Hannah's voice suddenly pounds. *Are you working with him now?*

Leave me alone. He's against the Network.

I used to think you were against the Network. Remember? You were going to shut it down.

up to Seventy

speeding it up

He's making a plan. I might not have to.

Jesus, you need your own Endgame Warning. You can't see what's right in front of you.

You're just making it harder.

"I think I was five," you say, blinking your eyes to clear your mind. "He burned my hand on the stove."

"Why?"

"They were seven dollars."

"What?"

"My gloves, I mean. I lost my gloves. They were seven dollars. He said I'd remember the next ones."

Sixteen just filed. Did you see?

Yeah. That kid's moving up.

I don't know, sounds like he failed to follow orders.

Doesn't matter. He cares more than any of us. He wants to win.

You laugh. Did you really think they'd left?

"Laika?"

Get it together and end it, all right?

I'm working on it.

You need to stop talking to Graham. He's lying again.

Then what does it matter? He'll be eliminated soon.

Make a plan, and shut it down.

"Laika?"

"What?"

"You were gone for a long time."

"What?"

"When I was talking to you. You weren't answering."

"I can't listen to everyone."

He nods. "I know."

You look around the room and everything seems covered in a haze. Like that time in the factory. You see he's put the clocks back up in slightly different places. The ticking sounds like teeth grinding. You shake your head. Graham's asking questions again, but it sounds like there are three or four of him talking at once and you can't understand what he's saying. You lie down on the couch and cover your ears and close your eyes. You need something— just one thing—to get out of your head. Eventually you can't hear him so you open your eyes and he's gone, but you see he put a blanket over you. You sit up and feel a little better. You take the batteries out of the clock in the living room. You relax.

I will shut it down, you think vaguely. *Maybe before Graham gets eliminated.* You laugh. You fall asleep.

62

There's a hush in the room and you suppose it's because they're expecting him. The light is low and you're not sure if Hannah's here. You stand at the back. No one seems to notice you. Two men in the last row are whispering, then one pushes his friend, smiling.

"I swear to God, it wouldn't have made a difference," he says.

"So that's why you turned off your murmur?" his friend laughs.

"You see up there? With the curls?" He's pointing to a woman close to the front.

"Yeah?"

"Seventy-Two."

"?"

"That's why I turned off my murmur."

You see Dev, up at the front. He's reading a book. A few others look familiar; you've seen them on the street. You don't see Graham.

Your dad walks in.

One Hundred.

From the front, across the stage, facing everybody.

His hair is the same, his beard. He looks more muscular, though, like he's been working out. He's got a big gun on a strap casually slung over his shoulder. You suppose it's an M-16.

"You guys," he begins with a sigh, "this isn't working."

People dart glances at each other but nobody says anything. You move a little farther back, into the shadows.

"I picked the best operatives back in July," he continues. "I thought it was an easy job. A way for you all to earn some credit."

His voice is low and gravelly, like he's sick. You remember his voice would lower when he said something in Russian. Yedinsvinaya. He learned it for her.

"But it looks like a stupid kid got the best of you."

He locks eyes with you. He winks.

"A really stupid kid."

He tosses something to Dev, a lighter, maybe, then moves the other way across the stage.

"You," he says, pointing to the woman with the curls, motioning for her to stand up. "Who are you?"

"Seventy-Two, sir."

"And what's your status?"

"Four months active, ground agent."

"Reports on file?"

"Twelve."

He frowns. "You've received a formal rebuke, is that right?"

She pauses. "Yes, sir."

"And what was that for?"

"Negative sightings."

"How many?"

"Three."

He shakes his head. "Three negative sightings. That's some shit. Well, really," he laughs, "that's some sabotage."

You run.

You get through three sets of doors before you hear the shots. You keep running, into the snow. The snow is pounding on you and it's everywhere you look. You don't know where you are but you keep running. You run but another second later you look and you're

back in Graham's apartment. The living room, the grinding clock. The clock. You already took out the batteries. It shouldn't do that. You look around.

You realize you can move like Hannah does. You're in on the meetings now. But you don't want to go back.

I told you it was bad.

How far did he go?

Seventy-Three. Just two tonight.

Do you know before there's an elimination?

"No," Hannah says, suddenly behind you.

You turn around and she's in Graham's armchair. Superman pajamas, with a cape.

"You don't get a warning?" you press, frowning.

"No." She looks at the clock shell and batteries on the floor. "I know you're trying to save Graham. It won't work."

"Because he left the Network?"

"Because they're all getting killed!" she exclaims. "Even the loyal ones, remember? And it won't be long."

"But I'm in on the meetings now."

"So?"

"So, maybe I can do something."

"You're in on the meetings so he can scare you. He wants you to see what he's capable of."

"Why? What will that do? It doesn't make any sense."

Hannah shrugs. "That's what makes it hard."

"What would you do?" you ask after a moment.

"Forget Graham."

"You still think this is part of his plan?"

"It doesn't matter." She pulls out her cigarettes. "You lose focus, you lose."

She hands you one and you take it slowly.

"Are you ten yet?"

"Yeah, just a few days ago. Thanks for asking." She lights both cigarettes.

"So, what should I be focused on?"

"What?"

"You said I can't lose focus. What am I supposed to be focused on?"

She gives you a look.

I'm being stupid again.

I'll say. You want me to draw you a map or something?

Fuck off.

"That's how you talk to a friend?" Hannah laughs. "We've been over this and over this."

You look at your watch but it's hard to read the time. You don't know if it's day or night.

"The Network," you sigh. "Shut down the Network."

She nods.

"I know," she says, adjusting her cape. "It's all we seem to talk about anymore."

Chapter 63

Graham

We Surrender to Win

It had been nearly ten minutes, but Graham couldn't stop staring at the number. He'd set aside the whole morning for this. He knew Laika wouldn't be up before eleven and he just wanted it over with. But he couldn't call the number. It was a lot easier than he'd thought to get it, and now he wasn't ready to follow through.

Graham picked up the phone on his nightstand but looked at the number again and felt his blood pressure rise. He couldn't lose it. Not this time. He hung up and leaned against the headboard. It was probably too easy. The hard part was three days earlier when he'd gone through her journal again, this time while she took a shower. He'd scanned the pages, looking for her to name anything—a school, a fast food joint, a mall. Toward the middle he found it: her friend said to meet at Sam Brannan. Graham looked into it and found it was a park in Yuba City.

He heard something, like a rustling out in the living room, so he got out of bed and softly moved to the door. She must have been shifting in her sleep because when he got to the living room he saw she was still buried in blankets, her breathing low and steady.

He sighed and returned to his bedroom. He needed to know more—to have something concrete for his meeting tomorrow with Anna's friend. And, inexplicably, Graham needed to hear him. *I've just got to do it.* He sat on the bed and picked up the phone, leaning over his nightstand so he could read the number. There was only one Casey Ephrem in Yuba City. This was it. He punched in the number.

It rang eleven times.

"Who's this?" a gravelly voice finally barked. He sounded drunk and half asleep and exactly as Graham had expected.

"Casey?" He tried not to sound like a dick right off the bat, but he couldn't keep the coldness out of his voice.

"No," the guy sighed, "for the last fucking time, this is his fucking brother, Dylan."

"Casey's not there?"

"No," Dylan groaned, and Graham heard what he was certain was the clanking of bottles. "But be sure to try back in twelve to eighteen months."

Graham paused. "He's in jail?"

"Bingo."

"What for? When was this?"

"Hey, I'm not his fucking lawyer," Dylan snapped. "Who are you, anyway?"

"Just a friend."

"Some friend," he laughed. "When's the last time you saw him?"

Graham held his breath, trying to think of a logical answer.

"I don't know, maybe three months ago," he said vaguely. "We'd meet up at the bars sometimes."

"Well, he won't be welcome at the bars anymore." Dylan chuckled and Graham got the feeling he was enjoying this.

"That's how he got in trouble?"

"All I know is he got into it with some guy at Paxton's, and then the cops found a lot of coke on him."

"And you're holding the apartment till he gets out?"

"Something like that."

Graham paused. "What happened to his daughter?"

There was silence for a moment and he began to panic. This guy could be dangerous, too.

"Staying with relatives," Dylan finally said. His voice was even, deliberate. "Does Casey owe you money or something?"

"Yeah, he does," Graham said, trying to sound pissed. "He owes me a lot of fucking money."

"Well, he'll make good on all his debts when he gets out. That's his official statement."

"I hope so."

"Just tell your friends he's in jail so they'll stop calling me, all right? It's driving me crazy."

"You bet."

Graham hung up quickly. He rubbed his face and his hands came back quivering. He was getting in over his head and starting to wonder if he was helping her at all.

Graham arrived at the medical building off Freelander the next day, still anxious from his exchange with Dylan, and feeling guilty for telling Laika he was working a long shift.

"Dr. Peretz?" he said, walking into the spacious corner office. "Thanks so much for seeing me."

"Please—Hadar," she said, rising to shake his hand. "And it's no trouble at all."

She motioned for him to sit across from her in a cushy chair upholstered in gray corduroy. Graham was suddenly hit with a sense of dread. He knew this meeting was for Laika, but still couldn't help running his own story through his head, choosing what to downplay and what to omit, wondering how much he should reveal in the first session.

"Anna's given me a general idea of the situation," she continued, "but your perspective is going to be especially helpful."

"I hope so."

Peretz did not look at all like he'd imagined. He had pictured someone Anna's age, but she was much older. Her long hair was curly, mostly silver, and much of it was covered by a red beaded scarf. Her office felt casual, almost homey, and there were personal touches everywhere. A photo of her family on the windowsill. A child's artwork on the wall. A colorful glass piece on her bookshelf shaped like the palm of a hand. He felt a bit better.

"So," she said, uncapping a pen and holding it near her blank notepad, "Laika is living with you, correct?"

"That's right."

"She trusts you?"

"I wouldn't say that. It comes and goes, I guess."

"And it seems this other world she experiences is extremely stressful."

"Yes."

"Okay. Anna tells me her delusions largely revolve around numbers, would you say that's still true?"

Graham nodded. "Clocks, and the people she calls the Numbers."

"Can you tell me more about them? The people in this other world?"

"They're all part of the Network," he said, watching as she wrote. "Her dad, Casey, is in charge of it, and he's One Hundred. The others work for him, and the more important they are to the Network, the higher their numbers. She thinks I'm Seventy-Seven."

"Why Seventy-Seven?"

"I don't know."

"Is that a number she could have seen around your apartment? Something written down? Is it on a shirt or a hat?"

"No, I don't think so. I mean, she thought I had a tattoo on my neck that said Seventy-Seven, but she thinks all the Numbers have tattoos."

"Is there anything else she says they all have in common?"

He frowned, trying to scroll back through all their conversations, all the notes he'd made. He dug the folded pieces of paper out of his pocket.

"Watches," he said finally, reading. "They communicate using their watches."

"And her dad is using this Network to find her—to bring her back?"

"Right." Graham sorted through his other notes. "I found out he got sent to jail recently, though."

"Why?"

"It sounded like a bar fight and cocaine possession. I got the number for his apartment and his brother answered."

"Why did you call him in the first place?"

"I really don't know," he smiled, embarrassed. "I guess I thought if I talked to him I might get something—some detail—to help her. And I thought about pretending to be police, just to get him nervous, you know? Let him know somebody's watching. So maybe if she ever did end up back with him, he'd be too scared to hurt her again."

Dr. Peretz nodded, made a few more notes then narrowed her eyes thoughtfully.

"Are there any other real people she claims are Numbers?"

Graham felt his body tense. "Just one, I think. Dev."

"Who's Dev?"

"She lived with him and a few others for a couple weeks. She ran away from my place and . . ." He looked away. "She found this group."

"Did you meet Dev?"

He nodded, looking past her out the window. He was getting the same feeling he always had in Dr. Schwartz's sessions. Like he was going to far, giving her too much. "I stopped him from trying to rape her."

Peretz stopped writing and looked up. She looked pained, like it was awful to think about but too common for her to work up much surprise over.

"Good for you," she said, meeting his eyes directly. "That's usually not how it ends."

"But I think he's done it before," Graham continued, his voice strained. "Or at least done something. I saw marks on her."

"Did she say anything about it?"

"No."

"Are you concerned about a possible pregnancy?"

Graham looked up, startled. He'd never considered it.

"I don't think she's hit puberty yet," he muttered, taking a breath and trying to bring down his temperature.

"She told you that?"

"One time she said she thought she might be getting her first period, but nothing happened."

Peretz nodded. "Under stressful conditions, a delay like that is fairly common. But she never confirmed about Dev?"

"I'm sorry?" Graham frowned, trying to focus. He wanted to kill Dev all over again. And he felt self-conscious, talking about this with someone he'd never met. He couldn't even do it with Schwartz.

"Your suspicions about Dev. She never confirmed?"

"No. She's focused on his role in the Network."

"What number is he?"

He paused. "Sixteen."

"But wouldn't that mean he's not very important?"

Graham shook his head. "He's the biggest threat. I guess he was recruited as a replacement for the Sixteen who was eliminated, but she said he's a natural. That everyone else is nervous because he's going to move up and take their numbers."

"And what about you? Are you a threat?"

"No," he replied with a faint smile. "I guess I was kind of a double agent trying to help her—I wasn't loyal to the Network." He paused. "And she said I'm in the next group to be eliminated."

"Is she worried for you?"

"I don't know. But I don't think she's scared of me anymore. She was at the beginning."

"Because she thought you were loyal to her father?"

He nodded. "It seemed like I was a bad guy for a while."

"Did you try to talk her out of her delusions?"

"At first. I tried to tell her the things she was seeing and hearing weren't real. That I was trying to help her."

Peretz nodded. "That's what our instincts tell us to do. To bring the people we care about back to normal." She set her pen down. "But unfortunately, that's what often drives them farther away. Sometimes it's actually better to go along with them, to learn as much as we can about what they're experiencing. Otherwise they pull away. And we could become menacing figures ourselves."

"I've started to realize that."

"Is that why she ran away from you?"

Graham felt his face redden again. He shifted in his chair and glanced around for a clock. There wasn't one. "No. She found out I'm an alcoholic. My sponsor called while I was at work."

"So you're a recovering alcoholic."

"Anna never told you that?" he asked with a questioning smile. "I mean, you're friends and everything."

She shook her head. "Nope. She never told me."

"Okay."

"Why did this make her run away?"

"I think her dad's an alcoholic," he continued, "and extremely violent. I think she was afraid she'd gotten herself into the same situation again."

"How did you get her to come back with you again?"

"I tried telling her the truth—how I've been in recovery for nine years and was never like Casey, but it didn't even seem to register. So I told her that if Dev is the biggest threat within the Network, she needs to get away from him."

Peretz looked past him thoughtfully.

"So, Dev's Sixteen, you're Seventy-Seven, and her father's One Hundred. What about the people who aren't real? Does she talk to them regularly?"

"She mostly listens to them, I think. But there is a girl, Hannah, she talks to. She gives Laika advice."

"So she's not a Number?"

"No," he shook his head. "But she knows a lot. She's in on the meetings."

"Does she give Laika orders?"

"I think so, sometimes. I think she can be kind of intimidating."

She nodded, then put down her pen again.

"I'd like to see her soon."

Graham felt his pulse pick up. "You think she's in trouble?"

"I think without treatment, the amount of time she spends in this other world will only increase. And that is very dangerous."

Graham nodded slowly. "I know."

He'd thought about it before—how it seemed to be getting harder and harder for her to pull herself back to reality.

"I'll talk to her," he said. But he knew that would be the hardest part.

64

It's raining. The air is thick, but cool, and you zip your jacket as you stand underneath the awning of the apartment complex. You bend down and touch the damp cement, just to check, to make sure it's really there.

"Why are we out here?" you ask finally, turning to Graham. He's standing next to you.

"To bring you back."

You gaze out at the rain, taking a deep breath.

"How long was I gone?"

Graham turns to you with a sad look, as if he doesn't want to tell you. His clothes are dirty and he nearly has a full beard.

"You hadn't said anything to me in nearly two days. I mean, you were talking, but not to me."

You nod.

"Anyway, it seems like being outside, it's almost like a reset. It can snap you out of it. That's why we're here."

"Sometimes I can't get back."

"I know."

"There's just so much to do, you know? There isn't any time."

"I know."

It's wet, but you sit on the steps and Graham sits next to you. You feel bad you left him for so long. Honestly, you kind of forgot about him. The Network's just been so much on your mind, and you're confident now Graham's no longer a part of it. But he'll still need your help.

"I made an appointment," he says, cracking his knuckles, "to see a doctor."

"For me?"

"Yeah."

And he's back in the game.

No. No way.

One last shot at saving himself. Can you blame him?

Not him.

"What kind of doctor?"

He pauses. "A psychiatrist. A friend of mine. She might be able to help keep you here more, so you don't have to deal with the Numbers all the time."

"How do you know she's not a Number? What if my dad's got control of the hospital?"

You start to sweat even though you know Hannah's wrong about him.

"Think about it," he says gently. "How many Numbers are really left? There can't be more than thirty, right?"

You haven't wanted to tell him, so you keep quiet, but he's watching you and thinking you must not know what you're talking about. He still thinks the outside is safe.

"Twenty-three," you say. "There are twenty-three left."

"Okay," he replies brightly, "so the chance of this doctor being a Number is tiny. Nothing to worry about."

"Graham," you murmur, frowning, "it means you're next. He killed Seventy-Six last night."

You're not cut out for this.

"Oh," he says softly.

He's quiet. You're sorry you told him. You still want to run.

"You really shouldn't worry about me."

"But you're next."

"I told you, remember? I won't let anything bad happen." He smiles and you think maybe he has a plan. Some way to avoid elimination.

"I thought you meant to me."

He laughs. "Well I won't do you much good if I can't take care of myself."

"Do you have a gun?"

"No."

"Then how are you going to stop him?" You're starting to get frantic. "He's not playing around, and he means what he says. There isn't much more time."

Graham frowns. "Have you heard him recently? Does he talk to you?"

You avoid his eyes but ultimately nod.

"He said he's got what he needs. That he doesn't care about the Network. He's going to kill the rest of the Numbers then take me back."

"Do you believe him?"

"Hannah thinks he's saying that so I'll give up trying to shut it down."

"How would you shut it down?"

"I don't know."

It's a lie, but he can't know. If there's even a slight chance he's still working for your dad, this would ruin you.

"Did he say anything else?"

"He says we have . . ." You let your sentence run out. You rub your eyes. ". . . we have to make up for lost time."

Graham doesn't say anything.

"I know he'll kill me," you continue, "it just sounds like he's going to draw it out."

"No," he declares. "No. Nothing is going to happen, okay? We'll go see this doctor, all right? She'll help us figure it out."

"A doctor can't do anything. It's already done."

"What's already done?"

"Everything. Everything is happening just like he said it would. None of the Numbers have been able to escape elimination. Why would a doctor help?"

It's another plant, all right? Stop trusting him.

He's trying to help.

He's trying to win.

Graham's looking at you pointedly, so you think he must have said something.

"A friend of yours?" you ask, frowning.

"That's right."

"You made an appointment?"

"Yeah, but it's really informal. No paperwork. Nobody has to know about it."

"They always know."

He shrugs. "We'll figure it out."

"When is it?"

"Thursday."

"And what's today?"

"Monday."

He thinks he'll be alive in three days.

Maybe he will.

I guess that's up to you.

65

You try to stay with him at dinner, but all you can think about is shutting down the Network. There's been a pause—a delay in the eliminations—but you know it's on purpose. Your dad's going to kill Graham in some spectacular fashion because he's become important to you.

"Do you think we could try that?" Graham's saying. You look up.

"What?"

"Writing down some of the things you hear. So we can keep track of what's going on."

You blink a few times.

"To give the doctor," you say slowly.

"It could help."

You shake your head. "I write a lot of stuff down, but it's not for her."

He nods. "Okay."

You look down. Graham made you the TV dinner you'd bought at Harry's. You're not sure what it is and you only vaguely remember buying it. You poke at it a little with your fork.

Is everyone here? I know it's short notice.

Yeah. We're all here. Except Seventy-Seven, of course.

"Laika."

You look up, a little startled because you seldom hear your name anymore. Graham looks tense. He rubs his eyes then runs his hands through his hair.

"I want to tell you something."

"All right."

It's going to be all of us. At once.

When?

Tomorrow night.

What about him?

He'll be gone before then.

You yell for Hannah in your mind, but she doesn't answer. You look at Graham.

"I need your help," he says. It's hard to hear him over the Numbers. "I thought I could do this by myself but I can't."

"Help with what?"

Where'd you get this intel?

Ninety-nine.

"I need you to shut down the Network."

You frown. "I told you I'm working on it."

He shakes his head and his eyes brim with tears.

"He's going to kill me, Laika. I heard them say it. I know you have a plan."

Why are you losing your shit?

Hannah, where have you been? He's planned the last elimination.

I know.

?

I just got out of the meeting.

"Please," he begs, leaning across the table. "Shut it down."

You rub your temples and try to think. It's all happening fast now. By tomorrow night you'll be the only one left.

"I'll figure it out," you mutter. Your heart's racing.

"The new code?" Graham asks, frowning. "No, you can't punch in random numbers; it'll lock you out of the building. Just keep this in your pocket if you don't think you can remember it."

He hands you a slip of paper. 88214. You look at him warily. Then Hannah jolts you back.

He's an idiot.

He's never heard the Numbers before. It scared him.

You really care about saving him?

It saves me, too.

I know. It's a good plan.

So what's the problem?

Just want to make sure you're doing it for the right reasons.

"I should go to bed," you whisper. Graham suddenly takes your hand.

"He'll make it worse for me, won't he?" he asks anxiously. "Not like the others. He'll torture me. I was never loyal."

"I know."

"But you have a plan."

You nod. "Yeah." Light is shimmering on the table from a window you never noticed before. "Yeah, I'll take care of it."

You know you can't fuck him, right? It was gross enough with Dev . . .

You ignore Hannah and head to the living room. You slide the blankets to the floor and lie down. You pull your bag close and unzip it. Instant coffee, a few blunts from Josie, some oranges and granola bars. Your journal. You pull it out and zip the bag up, tossing it aside. Graham's clinking plates together, clearing the table. You can tell he's trying to be quiet. You write the note. You clutch your journal and wrap yourself up in the blankets. You fall asleep to a faint buzz and the sound of Graham washing dishes.

66

He's coming. He's on his way.

The words are whispered so faintly you can barely hear them, yet they woke you out of a dead sleep. You shake your head and squint toward the kitchen, reading the digital clock over the microwave. 12:59. You'd only meant to lie down for a minute—to rest and clear your thoughts. Now it's dark and still and you're disoriented.

You said it wouldn't happen until tonight.

Not for us, dumbass. The kidnapping. He's coming for Seventy-Seven.

So, we still have time.

To get our affairs in order, I guess.

You jump up, suddenly alert. You're still holding your journal. Your hands are shaking. He's right; you still have time, but it's not going the way you wanted. Everything's rushed now. The note you'd written and saved falls from between the first pages of the journal. At least you'd gotten that done. You pick it up and walk quietly down the hall to Graham's room.

back with Casey.

You haven't gone in since that day with the boxes and the letters and the harsh, red eyes, and the belt you were sure he was going to use on you. It still turns your stomach to think how mad he was, and how it was your own stupid fault. But it doesn't matter now. Whatever happens, none of it matters. You turn the knob silently and open the door just a few inches until you hear his breathing. It sounds heavy and regular so you open the door a little more and slip inside. It's darker so your eyes take a few seconds to adjust before you can make out the shadows and shapes of the room. You move to the dresser. You take a breath and hesitate a moment before gingerly setting the journal on top, the note resting on the cover. You exhale. It's time.

But instead of slipping out the door you walk over to his bed. You watch him for a minute even though it makes you uneasy to be this close. Even in his sleep he looks scared. He winces a little every few seconds, and his breathing is ragged. He knows. He's hearing more and more from the Numbers and now your dad thinks he can take everyone out and make Graham suffer as your inaugural punishment.

Just do it, already. He's on his goddamn way.

You smile. You'll miss Hannah.

You won't have to.

I don't think you can follow me.

I can go wherever I want. A lot of us can. You won't be alone this time.

You move silently out of his room and down the hallway to the bathroom. You flip the switch and the harsh fluorescent light burns your eyes as it illuminates the mirror in front of you, and you cover them in pain, watching a photographic negative of yourself dance across your eyelids.

Maybe we should help.

How? What the fuck does that even mean?

I don't know. I've always liked him.

Seventy-Seven?

Yeah.

Doesn't matter now.

Why? Is he there?

Just outside.

You open your eyes. You blink slowly and study your reflection in the mirror. Light trails fall in and out of your vision. Your hair is longer than you thought. And you look older.

A map? I will draw it for you.

You take the knife out of your pocket. You look toward the door. Graham would wake up for just a second before your dad knocked him out again. Then it would be days, maybe weeks in some bargain building, bleeding and mumbling that he has a daughter even though he should know that won't work on Casey because he has a daughter, too.

You frown and slice upward from your wrist, still focused on your reflection in the mirror.

Chapter 67

Graham

If the Cure Works,
Chances Are You Have the Disease

A sudden crash jolted Graham awake. He lay there a minute, thinking it might have been part of a nightmare. But he saw light. Faint light under his door. He stood slowly, trying to dispel the grogginess he felt. He rubbed his eyes and went for the door, but then he saw her journal. It was dark but he could tell what it was immediately, and it added to his confusion. *Maybe it's still a dream,* he thought, looking around to see what else might be out of place. He slid on his sweatshirt jacket. He switched his bedroom light on. He squinted and picked up the journal. There was a note on top. It was real. It was real and it shouldn't have been happening and his heart pounded as he read her jumbled handwriting.

> *Graham. Sorry about all this. He's coming for you now, they all said he'll do it tonight and I know you're listening now too so maybe you already know. But don't worry, I'm shutting down the Network before he can get here, I hope. Hannah said I'm right and I know what to do now, so don't worry. Here's my journal because maybe there's something in it to help you if this doesn't work, and I know I owe you anyway. Don't tell Emerson anything. I don't want her in danger if this goes wrong.*

Graham was caught up in the letter and the journal, forgetting for a moment about the crash. But then his heart jumped and he stuffed the journal in his jacket pocket and sprinted out the door because he realized she must have done something definitive.

He saw the shattered ceramic bowl first, the strewn bottles of lotion. He opened the door wider and his breathing just stopped, like the air had been sucked out of his lungs. He couldn't move. Graham saw Laika lying in her own splattered blood, the pocket knife next to her, but then the metal exploded and all he could see was that black field and a haze of smoke blotting out the stars. He heard the people shouting at him, begging for help, and felt himself sink to his knees as the pressure in his stomach increased.

No.

He looked at her again and still heard the chaos, but felt something stronger begin to pound through his veins.

Graham struggled to get to his feet, wiping his eyes. He ran to the kitchen phone and dialed 9-1-1. He held the doorframe as his shaking legs threatened to buckle. Hysteria seeped into his head and he wasn't sure what he was even saying to the dispatcher, but she seemed to grasp the enormity and told him they'd be right over.

He ran back to Laika, falling again to his knees, trying to think of something to do. She'd only cut one wrist. He wasn't sure if it was still bleeding, but he wrapped a t-shirt from the floor around it tightly. He felt her neck for a pulse, but he didn't know what he was doing and couldn't feel anything. There was blood matted into her hair and it looked like she'd hit the back of her head when she lost consciousness and fell. Graham put his hand in front of her mouth and thought he could feel her breath. He waited a minute until he was sure it was there. It was intermittent and shallow and he started to lose control again.

He was breathing too fast and thought he might pass out. The smoldering train and the people on fire forced their way back into his mind. The smoke burned his eyes and sickened his stomach. He thought about all his sleepless nights, about the matches he couldn't even light.

"No."

Graham gently lifted her into his arms, making sure the t-shirt was still in place around her wrist, and walked resolutely out the door because he was tired of himself and he wasn't going to let some visions keep him from helping her. He carried her out of the apartment and down the stairs, knowing the ambulance would come north up Prospect from the hospital on 112th and maybe he could meet it on the way.

He was walking fast and nobody was out, and when they passed underneath a streetlight he noticed something. A bracelet. Laika was wearing a bracelet on her other wrist—just like the one he wore. It was from Emerson, made with yellow and pink braided rubber bands. He started to cry. He wanted to tell her all the things he was thinking now. He was shaking and crying and it was hard to breathe, but it wasn't long before he looked up to see the red and white ambulance lights flashing ahead of him.

68

"I knew you'd be back," you suddenly hear from behind you. You turn to see Hannah, in footed, jellybean pajamas, smiling as she pushes through the double doors of the meeting hall.

"How did I get here?"

She shrugs and gives you a silly look that seems to suggest you're asking too much of a ten-year-old. You look around. It's set up just like last time—rows of chairs with people sitting and talking to each other, a nervous energy flying between them. You shake your head.

"They know, right? I mean, why would they show up when they know it's for elimination?"

"They have to."

"Why?"

"What do you think elimination looks like for the ones who don't show up?"

You immediately think of Graham.

"Is he okay?"

But Hannah's looking past you. The Numbers are starting to get up. They're whispering in groups of twos and threes, like they're trying to get their facts straight, looking at you, pointing at you, and smiling incredulously at each other.

"Hannah . . ." you begin warily, still watching as they begin to approach.

"Don't worry," she murmurs. "You did it."

"What?"

"You shut down the Network. And they just figured it out."

You look at her squarely. "It's over?"

"Hey," one of them begins timidly, coming over and pushing his glasses up the bridge of his nose. "I'm Eighty-Three. Well, I guess I'm just Max now." He smiles. "Thank you."

The rest come up and start murmuring their thanks, shaking your hand, telling you their real names. Hannah stands back and lights a cigarette. You're not sure what to do.

"So," another one ventures, "how . . ." She pauses, looking around as if Casey might burst into the room any second. "How did you do it?"

This starts the room clamoring. They all want to know. They're laughing easily now, talking excitedly to you and each other like they've just awoken to realize their death sentence was only a bad dream. A middle-aged man, probably from the nineties, speaks up, commanding the room to settle down. He takes your hand and leads you to the front, up on the stage.

"It's fine now," he whispers, his hand on your shoulder. "All they want is to know it's real."

"It is real."

"Good," he smiles. "Tell them."

"Were you Ninety-Nine?" you ask.

"That's right. And now I'm Harvey."

He turns you around to face the others. They're standing together, expressions of pure relief still etched on their faces.

"Everyone," you begin cautiously. "The Network is gone."

They all cheer. You smile but you're still not sure what to do. They clap and holler and a few call out, "But how? How did you shut it down?"

"I, well . . ." you run your hands over your hair. You glance at your wrist but there's nothing there. "I just . . . wait." You suddenly stop, surveying their faces, your heart beginning to pound. You don't see Graham. "Wait just a second." He should be in on this now. He should be okay. But what if you were too late? Your voice gets louder. "Where is he? Does anyone know where Casey is right now?"

"One Hundred?" Harvey asks, puzzled. "He'll be long gone by now. In hiding, if he's lucky."

"But how can you be sure?" you demand, getting frantic. "Has anyone heard anything to confirm that?"

They look at each other, all of them confused now.

"He's probably dead," another one offers. "He had a lot of enemies."

You rub your forehead. "But we need to know for sure," you say, pleading. "We need to know—"

Then you see him.

Graham.

Standing at the back, just inside the doors. His crazy hair and scruffy face, still wearing the t-shirt and flannel pajama pants he'd been sleeping in. He smiles.

Only then do you start to believe your own words: the Network is gone. You get off the stage and the others are whispering to each other but you walk past them, your eyes clouding with tears as you realize just how hard you would have taken it if he'd been caught. Tortured. Eliminated.

But it's over. It's real and you don't have to hide anymore. You stand in front of him, wanting to say something about the letters and the journal and how you're sorry he'd gotten mixed up in all of this. But you don't say anything and the tears spill over. Graham hugs you and says he'll never be able to thank you enough for saving him and tells you everything's going to be different now.

The energy is nervous again. The Ex-Numbers are getting restless and you realize they don't want to be there anymore. They can't be in that place where so many eliminations happened, where so many orders were given, promises made and taken away. Hannah murmurs something to Harvey and he walks to the double glass doors, calling and motioning everyone out. You all follow and stand on the street. You look up at the streetlamp, snow flying crazily through the air, diffusing its light.

"What do we do now?" one of them asks. They all look at each other. They don't know what to do without orders.

"I know," Hannah pipes up. She steps out of the shadows and into the light. She digs through her sparkly silver purse until she finds her lighter. She tosses it to Graham. "You do it, Mr. Calley."

No one says anything. He looks up at the building. "Really?" he asks, but with a slight smile like he's just trying to make sure he won't get in trouble. He looks at Harvey, who nods silently.

"I've got my own, actually," he tells Hannah, handing back her lighter and pulling an orange matchbook out of his pocket.

You count the people on the sidewalk to make sure everyone's out. Graham walks back into the meeting hall with his matches. After a few minutes he comes back out and says it shouldn't take long.

"Let's cross," he adds, peering through the windows at the flames now creeping up the walls. You walk as a group across the vacant street and stand together on the sidewalk as snow rushes in front of your eyes and turns the meeting hall a diluted rust color as it burns.

"I'm sorry you had to end it that way," Graham says after a moment, turning to you. "I should have helped you."

"You couldn't. You weren't the target."

"I guess."

You look at him. He's wearing his gray jacket now but you don't know where it came from. You study his weary face carefully.

"You were never loyal?"

"No."

"Then why did you join in the first place?"
"I didn't; I was recruited. And I didn't want to be killed."
You nod. "Me either."

Chapter 69

Graham

Turn It Over

Graham had been waiting a long time. Almost two hours. He had to tell them he wasn't her father, that her real father was in jail now and she'd run away from him and she had this condition that was looking like paranoid schizophrenia, but nobody had really been able to diagnose her yet. He said she'd been trying to find her aunt . . . but at that point they didn't want to hear any more from him. He might get in trouble—they told him he should have filed for guardianship if she was going to stay with him—but none of that mattered now.

He was sitting in the waiting room with a few other people, facing the television set that was playing cartoons. It was nearly five a.m. He looked down. He still had her blood on his shirt. His eyes welled with tears and he had to look away. He needed a cigarette, but he wasn't allowed to smoke in the hospital and he couldn't light it anyway.

The journal was still in his hands. He'd read it, waiting for her. He started at the beginning, with the drawings and stories and short poems, and he'd smiled because it reminded him of Emerson and made him happy to think Laika was ever childlike. But even those were intermingled with dark dreams and desperate fantasies. Graham learned her mother had died years ago and that's when her father appeared to spiral. He read about the violence, which seemed to increase in frequency and severity over the last couple of years. That was when her entries started to change. She'd reported her experiences—time spent with her friends, things that went on at school, abuse from Casey—more factually, with very little emotion. It was gradual, maybe over the course of two years, but Graham now believed her illness was nonexistent, or at least latent, before then. He read her recent entries, distorted and confused. He read about Dev, and felt his muscles tighten. He had been right.

"Graham Calley."

He jumped up and followed Dr. Mata, the one who'd admitted Laika, but his heart sank when Mata led him to an empty exam room.

"Where is she?" he asked. "Is she okay?"

"She'll be fine," Mata replied, "but she won't be awake for a while. And I'd like to ask you a few things first."

Graham closed his eyes and rested his head in his hands. They hadn't been telling him anything. He wasn't sure if she'd make it. He was exhausted and scared, but now there was this weight off his heart and his whole body started to quiver.

"She's okay?" Graham repeated, practically laughing with relief. "You're sure?"

"Absolutely," the doctor smiled. "I know it looked like a lot of blood, but the cut missed the main artery, and wasn't deep enough to cause serious damage. She does have a concussion, though."

"What do I do for that?"

"Just make sure she gets lots of rest. No stressful or strenuous activities. And use an ice pack if you see any swelling."

Graham nodded and Mata looked at him carefully.

"She'll continue to stay with you, then?"

"Yes."

"Will you seek guardianship?"

"I can, if that's what she wants. I mean, she ran away to find her aunt, so I've been trying to locate her but there's not much to go on."

"You haven't talked to the police?"

"I didn't want them to send Laika back with her dad."

"They won't."

"How do you know?"

"You have her journal," Mata said. "She's documented the abuse, so even if she's unable to articulate it now, with her illness, we have evidence that says it happened."

Graham nodded. *He said "we."*

"I'll have to talk to them now, though," he continued, writing something down.

"What? The police?"

"Yes." Mata looked up. "I'm a mandated reporter. If I see something like this, involving a minor, I'm required by law to notify them."

"But what about the state? Couldn't they put her in juvenile detention or something?"

"That's why you should seek guardianship," he said firmly. "She's going to need an advocate."

"So, you think I did the right thing, bringing her in?"

"I've got four kids," he replied. "Of course I do."

Graham sat silently for a moment.

"Thank you," he finally murmured. He looked up at the clock. "They said a psychiatrist would come in soon."

He nodded. "Dr. Garcia. She specializes in schizophrenia." He reached for his notes. "You've already been speaking with a specialist, right?"

"A doctor my ex-wife works with. They'll both be here later this morning."

"Good," Mata replied. "We'll map out a treatment plan."

"And this is allowed?" Graham frowned. "I mean, I can sign off on meds for her, that kind of thing?"

"In this case, yes." Mata handed him some literature on schizophrenia. "As a general rule, we do what's in the child's best interest. With her only known living relative in jail, and with you in the process of becoming a legal guardian," he said evenly, looking at Graham over his glasses, "there are provisions."

Graham looked down at the pamphlets. His head was still reeling and the room felt smaller than it did a minute before and he just wished he could see her.

"But you should file soon, with the court," Mata said gently. "Get the paperwork started, anyway. It can all be changed later, if she ends up somewhere else."

"Sure," Graham nodded. He didn't want her to end up somewhere else.

"And use the police," Mata continued, rising from his seat. "They could help you find her aunt."

"Where are you going?" Graham stood as well, too quickly, then held the desk until the darkness receded.

"I've got a short break, then a few more patients to see. Don't worry," Mata smiled, "you'll see her as soon as possible. I'll come find you in the waiting room."

Graham nodded and followed him to the door.

"You're going on break?" he asked, fumbling in his pocket. "Do you smoke?"

70

You don't hear the Ex-Numbers for three days after you all disperse from the charred remains of the meeting hall. But on the fourth day, they contact you.

Devushka.

?

Sorry. Laika. This is Max.

Why are you doing this? There's no Network anymore.

But we've got him.

Your hands start to sweat and you get up off Graham's couch and start pacing the room. You just wanted it to be over.

How? How did you even find him?

He still had a working murmur on him; we could track it.

What do you want me to do?

. . .

Come on, Max—what?

Kill him.

Your heartbeat slams in your ears. You look around for Hannah or Graham, but she hasn't come around since the fire and he's working a double shift today. The clocks start grinding again and you feel like you're right back where you started.

I don't want to.

. . .

I'm serious. Find somebody else.

But . . . it's only fair, right? Everybody's been waiting for this but we saved it for you. I mean, with all you went through—

No.

Well, I guess we could let Ninety-Nine do it . . .

Harvey? Yeah, fine. That's fine.

All right. We'll have him do it tonight, then.

Wait, Max?

?
Can I talk to him first?
Harvey?
No. My dad.
Not like this. He's out of contact. You'll have to come down.

Hannah walks you to the warehouse on Matthias. The symmetry of it feels wrong, but you suppose they chose the location to make you feel more comfortable. You think about "Group 47" and wonder if the Numbers had anything to do with it. The window's been boarded up with plywood so you can't get in that way.

"We'll have to go around," you tell Hannah. "There's a back door."

"I'll wait," she says, sitting on the stoop and avoiding your eyes.

"You're not going in with me?"

"Just call if you need me, all right?"

You didn't think Hannah got scared like that, but you don't blame her.

"Sure."

You walk around and gently test the flimsy door, its wooden slats rotting away. It's unlocked. The air suddenly changes inside and it's damp and heavy, like a jungle. They've turned on the lights—those stark bare bulbs you always hated—and you follow their glow around the boxes and furnace and water heater to the open space. None of the Exes are there. But he's there.

"Laika."

He says your name flatly, like it's just another bothersome item on his to-do list. You take a breath. Max and Harvey and the others—they didn't show up. Maybe they still think you'll do it.

You force yourself to look at him. He's tied to a chair, hands behind his back. His face is already slightly bruised and smeared with blood. They couldn't even wait for you to talk to him. He watches you steadily but you don't know what to say.

"I didn't think you'd have the balls for this," he says finally.

"For what?"

"To kill me."

You frown. "I had the balls to shut down the Network." Smart-ass.

He laughs. "Okay."

"You killed a lot of people," you say quietly.

"Are you going to stay over there?" he asks, annoyed. "Because I can barely hear you." You realize you're still across the room from him. "I can't hurt you," he adds, as if that would make you feel better.

You walk closer to him, scanning the area for any possible sign that it's a trick. But his hands are tied, his feet are tied, and it doesn't matter anyway because you carried out your own elimination so he has nothing left. His t-shirt is torn and his jeans are dirty. He must have struggled when they brought him in. His hair is ragged and his beard is fuller than you remember. But he's still the same.

"You killed a lot of people," you repeat.

He shrugs. "I ran a company. And they stopped trying."

"All that to get me back?"

"I wouldn't think of it like that," he smiles. "I didn't really want you; I just couldn't have you talking."

You rub your eyes. "And you ordered Dev to sleep with me?"

"Of course."

Your stomach pitches. "He's twenty-three years old."

"So you noticed the age difference?" *your dad asks with amusement.* "Nine years. Same as your mother and me."

"That's sick."

"I bet he was good though, wasn't he?" *he continues.* "I've heard Indian dick is the best."

"Fuck you."

His body twists suddenly, like he's suffered an electric shock, but you realize it was just his natural reflex to hit you.

"He's dead now, too, you know."

You know this remark is meant to hurt you, but it doesn't. Your blood pressure's rising for a different reason. Your face is getting hot and your hands are sweating because it's obvious he doesn't care about any of it. Even in the face of his certain death he feels no remorse. And you know he'd do it all again in an instant.

"Do you remember that camping trip? With Brit?" *you ask abruptly.*

"Did you just come here to ask me stupid questions?"

"You told me I could go. You did. I didn't make it up and I know you remember."

He sighs. "We were never a team, Laika. I know that's what you were looking for, but you're just a dumb kid. Your mother and I were the team, and I got a shitty deal when she died."

You look down at the floor, trying to find some composure, when you suddenly notice something. Writing.

The Exes. They've written in chalk all over the concrete floor.

Monday: Harvey—drill, Tuesday: Carl—pliers, Wednesday: Marjorie—needles, Thursday: James—hammer . . .

Max lied to you; they're not doing it tonight. It goes on for weeks. Every Ex-Number, in descending order, gets to have a shot at him. You skip to the last one.

Tuesday: Laika—gun.

"Looks like fun, doesn't it?" *he asks, bringing you back.* "They're going to keep me pretty busy."

You narrow your eyes. He's not scared. You search his face, trying to figure it out. He's not scared and you don't know how that's possible. Unless he has a plan. You take a step back from him, feeling your pulse pick up.

"Why aren't you asking me to help you?"

"Why would I do that?"

"Because they're going to torture you for weeks." You gesture to the schedule on the floor. "It's going to be hell."

"Do you think my operatives—the Exes, as you call them—are really loyal to you now? You think they switched sides so easily?"

"You were killing them," you say slowly. "They want it to be over."

He shrugs. "Maybe I offered them something better."

"They're going to torture you," you repeat weakly.

He laughs. "Do you know what I was going to do to your boyfriend?"

"My boyfriend?"

"Seventy-Seven."

"He's not my boyfriend. He's nearly as old as you are."

"Well, you've always been a fucked-up kid."

"Doesn't matter; it's all over now."

He smiles. "Okay."

You feel in your pocket until your sweaty hand grips the knife you still carry. He has a plan and you don't think a few ropes holding him in a chair are going to get in the way. You click the blade open.

"I was going to keep him five, maybe six weeks," he continues, an eerie contentment in his eyes. "By the fourth day he'd be begging me to kill him."

"Looks like that's going to be you, now," you say as evenly as you can.

"And his daughter," he laughs. "I'd bring her in after a week."

Your heart stops and you feel cold. He knows about Emerson. Your whole body starts to shake.

His eyes meet yours. "I'd do all the things to her that I was planning to do to you."

"No," you shake your head. "It's all over." Your voice is strained and you're trying to convince yourself it's true. But he still has plans.

"She probably won't last more than a few days," he says, sounding disappointed. He's not talking in hypotheticals anymore. "But I'll see what I can do. You know, draw it out." He looks at you meaningfully. "Make up for lost time."

It's all over. You plunge the knife into his chest. Then you do it again.

Chapter 71

Graham

Just for Today

Graham convinced the doctors to let him into her room before she woke up. He said it would be better for her—that she was in a strange place and should see someone she knew when she woke up.

She looked so young, lying there, breathing easily and looking peaceful for once. He wasn't sure what he would say to her when she woke up.

Anna and Dr. Peretz came in after a while. Peretz said they wanted to start her on intravenous medication before she woke up, an antipsychotic that could begin to curb her hallucinations immediately. Graham told her that was fine, and after a few minutes Mata came back with Dr. Garcia and they had him sign a few forms. He handed them back and a nurse started working on the IV. Graham began talking with Garcia again, asking more about the pills she'd take, the evaluations and therapy she'd need. Garcia had brought more literature with her.

A few minutes later Laika stirred, so he turned back to her. She was moving her head and wincing a bit, like the room was too bright. Graham's heart raced as he pulled a chair close to her bedside, wanting to be near her, but worried she'd wake up and think he was in the Network again. Or she wouldn't recognize him at all.

"Laika," Graham said softly, studying her face.

Her eyes opened slowly, but then immediately widened as they took in the room. She sat up carefully and he knew she was starting to panic.

"Laika, it's me," he said calmly. "It's Graham."

Anna and the other doctors had moved into the background, which he appreciated, but she was looking at her bandaged wrist and the tape on her arm, and when she turned to him there was pure terror in her eyes.

"I killed him," she whispered. "I stabbed him in the chest."

"Who?"

"My dad." She looked toward the others cautiously. "He was in the warehouse. He told me he was going to torture you for weeks. He said he would find Emerson, too. The Ex-Numbers are still working for him; they're still in the Network and they've all been lying, and . . ." She couldn't catch her breath so Graham handed her a cup of water.

"No," he said evenly. "You were unconscious for a long time. You didn't kill anyone and nobody's after you. Casey's in jail."

"What?"

"He's been there for a couple of months. He's not after you."

Laika was just sitting there, maybe trying to work everything out, but her eyes were getting vacant. Graham wished he could make this easier for her.

"You have an illness," he said, "and it's hurting you. It created this other world that's making you afraid. But we know what the problem is now." He glanced back and Anna smiled at him. "We know what the problem is and we can fix it."

"I thought I shut down the Network," she said, staring blankly in front of her. "But he still had plans."

"I know it's hard," he said. "It'll take a while for this to make sense. But you're safe now, okay? And I'm not going anywhere."

She didn't say anything and kept staring at nothing. Graham wondered how much the medicine would really help her. He knew it wouldn't be perfect, that's what Garcia told him. She said they might have to try a few different medications and dosages before they found something that worked. He just wanted her to have some peace from all this.

"You want Emerson to come by later?"

Laika finally turned to him. She nodded.

"She's okay?"

"She's great," he smiled.

"Okay. How long am I going to be here?"

"I don't know. Do you want to talk to the doctors? You can ask them anything you want."

She looked past Graham and narrowed her eyes cautiously, but ultimately nodded again.

Garcia came over. She explained what was going on, and what would probably happen over the next few weeks. She was good, Graham decided, but he saw Laika scrutinizing her and he worried about what she was thinking—if she still suspected there were Numbers out to get her.

The others left within an hour and Graham stayed with Laika until late afternoon when she fell asleep again. He asked Garcia and Mata to let him know when she woke up and he'd come back. He didn't want her to be alone.

Graham walked out of the hospital. He stood in front of the building for a minute, unsure of what to do next. Before, as he was getting ready to leave, Mata had directed him to the bus stop outside the hospital entrance, telling him there should be another bus along in about ten minutes. He'd said "thanks" and thought about calling a cab, but he knew today he'd rather walk the long distance than talk to anyone else.

He trudged down Brooks Boulevard, past 103rd where Anna lived, wondering if she'd tell Emerson anything or leave it for him to explain. He still couldn't really think about it. And he was ashamed because he had felt himself slip. It had been a long time since he felt pulled by alcohol—since his relapse—but sitting in that hospital waiting room after he'd brought Laika in, he just wanted to make everything go away. Graham sighed. At least he'd have material for the next meeting.

After a while, he saw a young woman in front of a closed nightclub. She was probably in her late twenties, with blonde dreadlocks, smoking and reading the flyers stapled to the light post. Graham anxiously pulled his cigarette package out of his pocket.

"Excuse me," he said, walking over to her. "Do you have a light?"

She looked up and briefly scanned his appearance. He'd forgotten about the blood all over his shirt and jacket.

"I'm sorry," he said quickly, "this must look bad."

She smiled, digging out a lighter. "I've seen a lot worse."

She handed it to him. Just holding it made his hands sweat. Graham looked at it a moment and contemplated telling her he had changed his mind, that it was a bad habit and maybe he should quit, but he wanted it too badly.

"Sorry," he said again, giving her back the lighter. "I know this is weird, but I have a . . . well, a problem. With matches, lighters, that kind of thing. I can't light it myself."

"Oh. Were you in a fire or something?" she asked sympathetically, clicking the flame on.

"Yeah." He watched her hold it to his cigarette.

"I get it," she replied. "I was in a car accident a few years ago and I still can't listen to The Rolling Stones, because that's what was playing on the radio."

Graham nodded and took a long drag, starting to feel a little better.

"Thanks."

He looked down Eighty-First. The sun was starting to set. Only twenty more blocks to go.

"Thanks," he said again.

She shrugged. "We've all got something, I guess."

72

Graham says you didn't kill Casey. He says there's no Network. At first you think that's nice of him, trying to protect you, but he's persistent and you start feeling better and after a while you think maybe there's something to it. He says it's all part of an illness that's been growing, picking up steam these last few months. You haven't heard anything from the Numbers, and you don't have any direction from Hannah. You wake up thinking about Emerson, though. On the nights she's over you get up and check on her, check on Graham, then check the locks on the windows and doors. Most nights you check on Graham anyway.

"You want to go out today?" Graham asks you, a couple of weeks after you leave the hospital. You're eating lunch with him, and he says he's off work again today. That he's going to be off for a long time.

"Where?"

"Just out. You know, get some air. Then we can pick Emerson up."

"You think that's okay?"

He nods. "Remember, everything's different now."

You take a drink of coffee—Graham's good kind, not the instant. You've been eating his food again, too. You were worried at first, though, when you came home from the hospital and he showed you the pills. Pills you would need every day. Chemicals they'd already been giving you intravenously at the hospital. It could be anything, you'd said. But he showed you the bottles and asked you if you felt different—if there was less talking in your head, less worry about people watching you. He said the pills would help keep you here, separate you from the entire world of the Numbers—a world that only existed for you—and after a while you would feel in control. He said you'd meet with a doctor, too: Peretz or Garcia or anyone you'd like, every week to work on staying here. He told you he'd been through something similar; after the accident he'd seen buses crash and planes crash and buildings burn and people die, but it wasn't real. He said it took him a long time but he got past it and he wants to help you. And after everything that's happened, you can believe he's on your side.

"All right," you say, "let's go out."

The afternoon is bright and crisp and you walk with Graham to get Emerson from school. She's standing by the honeysuckle tree in front of Westmoreland Elementary where Graham likes her to wait. She lights up a little when she sees you're with him.

"Laika," she smiles.

She jogs toward you, her yellow backpack bouncing up and down. She stops a few feet away and holds her hand up, so you walk toward her and give her a high-five.

"Can we go to the park?" she asks. She's still looking at you, as if you're in charge.

"That's fine," Graham shrugs, "but I want to hear about your math test first."

"Math test first," she mutters, like she's trying to decode a message he's given her. She looks up. "I was the first one done."

"Oh, was it a race?"

"No."

"You should take your time."

She looks at him curiously. "I did."

It's nice out, but there aren't many people at the park. A couple of kids in the baby swings, a few middle schoolers playing soccer. Emerson heads for the monkey bars and Graham collapses onto the bench, his leg jittering. You know he wants a cigarette but he's been trying to cut back. You sit next to him.

"How long has it been?" you ask.

"Almost twenty-four hours."

"Maybe you need some of that gum."

He smiles. "Yes. I'd like a shit-ton of that gum right about now."

You don't see Emerson when you look over again, so you stand up and scan the equipment until you see her bright pink shoes sticking out of the play tunnel. You still picture Casey coming for her. Coming for all of you. It's a hard memory to dispel. You sit back down and Graham squeezes your shoulder, like he knows what you're trying to do.

"When does Lena get here?" you ask.

"Wednesday." He pauses. "Six days."

You think about this and breathe in deeply. You're not sure how you feel about it now. It was a relief for sure when they found her—Graham and the police he'd been working with—back in Novgorod. She'd cried on the phone when Graham told her everything that was going on, and she'd booked a ticket to California the same day. But as the days pass and her arrival date approaches you're getting nervous. Maybe she's not at all like what you imagine.

"Do you think she'll stay?"

"For good?" He looks at you but you can't read his face.

"Yeah."

"She might." He squints into the sun. "She might ask you to go back with her to Russia."

You already know that, but your pulse quickens anyway.

"When are you going back to work?" you ask, watching the playground again.

"I'm not in a rush," he replies.

You're about to ask him more about it when you hear a voice from behind you, calling you. You turn around.

"Laika, hey."

It's strange to see Hannah in regular clothes—jeans and a faded t-shirt. She's wearing sunglasses and her hair is in pigtails. She smiles and waves you over.

"I need to talk to you."

You get up.

"Are you okay?" Graham asks, watching you carefully.

You nod. "I'll be right back."

You walk with her to a tree about thirty feet away. She nods to Graham.

"How's he doing?" she asks.

"Fine," you reply, glancing over at him. He turns back to watch Emerson. "I think everything's fine."

"Good."

"Do you know what happened to him?" you ask carefully.

"Casey?"

"Yeah."

"I don't know." She pauses. "I haven't heard anything."

"Graham says he's been in jail."

"Sounds about right."

You hear a shriek so you look over but it's just some other kids, playing tag.

"Are you still in on the meetings?"

"There aren't any more meetings."

"Do you think the Exes—the Numbers—are back together, looking for me?"

"It's possible," she says, "but I think I would have heard." She adjusts her sunglasses. "We still have to be careful, though."

You take a breath. "Graham says it's not real." Hannah shrugs. "Is that true?"

"I guess anything's possible."

You nod. You don't feel much of anything.

"So, anyway," she begins, pulling her cigarettes out of her pocket, "I just wanted to check on you. See how everything's going." She clicks the lighter and holds a cigarette to the flame.

"Thanks."

Hannah smiles, looking past you. "He's trying to quit, isn't he?" she asks, gesturing to Graham who's drumming his fingers on the bench while his leg still jitters.

"Yeah," you look back, feeling a rush of fondness for him. "It'll be tough."

"Isn't everything?"

"Has been so far."

"Don't worry," she says. "You're doing fine."

"So, I'll see you around?"

She sighs, like she always did when you were being stupid, but doesn't say anything.

You smile and turn away. You go back to the bench and sit down next to Graham. He's nervous.

"You saw someone," he says slowly.

"Yes."

"Are you all right?"

"Yeah."

"Who was it?"

"Hannah."

"Did she want you to do anything?"

"Not this time. She was just checking on me."

Graham lets out a deep breath. "I think that's okay."

"You think it's really over now?"

He shakes his head. "Remember, it won't be perfect; we can't expect everything to go away completely. And it'll take time—a couple months, at least. But you will feel better, and you've got a lot of people to help you."

You rub your head, your mind still keeping the pieces apart, not allowing it to make sense to you. But you trust Graham, and that feels like progress.

"That long?" you ask, glancing behind you.

"Don't worry," he smiles, gazing out at the playground. "It'll go by before you know it."

You nod and look out toward the playground as well, your muscles relaxing once you spot Emerson.

About the Author

Kate Kort was born in St. Louis, Missouri, in 1985. She studied English and world literature at Truman State University. She currently lives in a suburb of Portland, Oregon, with her husband and three children. Some of her favorite authors include Salman Rushdie, G.K. Chesterton, Carl Hiaasen, Mikhail Bulgakov, Andrei Bely, and Arundhati Roy.

Glass (2015, Brick Mantel Books) was her debut novel.

www.KateKort.com

CPSIA information can be obtained
at www.ICGtesting.com
Printed in the USA
LVOW08s0619191017
552968LV00008B/158/P